A Book Of

LABOUR WELFARE

For
M.P.M. Part I – Semester – II
Effective from June 2013

Prof. Sharad D. Geet
M A. (Eco), M.Com, LLB
Nashik

Mr. Amit D. Deshpande
B.E. (Production), M.B.A.
General Manager
Sai Associates, Satara

Mrs. Asmita A. Deshpande
B.Com, M.B.A.
Manager (Finance), Ankur Industries,
Pune

NIRALI PRAKASHAN
ADVANCEMENT OF KNOWLEDGE

N2986

MPM - Sem. II : Labour Welfare   **ISBN 978-93-83750-7**

Second Edition   :   **January 2016**

©   :   **Authors**

Published By :

NIRALI PRAKASHAN

Abhyudaya Pragati, 1312, Shivaji Nagar,

Off J.M. Road, PUNE – 411005

Tel - (020) 25512336/37/39, Fax - (020) 25511379

Email : niralipune@pragationline.com

☞ DISTRIBUTION CENTRES

PUNE

Nirali Prakashan   :   119, Budhwar Peth, Jogeshwari Mandir Lane, Pune 411002, Maharashtra
Tel : (020) 2445 2044, 66022708, Fax : (020) 2445 1538
Email : bookorder@pragationline.com, niralilocal@pragationline.com

Nirali Prakashan   :   S. No. 28/27, Dhyari, Near Pari Company, Pune 411041
Tel : (020) 24690204 Fax : (020) 24690316
Email : dhyari@pragationline.com, bookorder@pragationline.com

MUMBAI

Nirali Prakashan   :   385, S.V.P. Road, Rasdhara Co-op. Hsg. Society Ltd.,
Girgaum, Mumbai 400004, Maharashtra
Tel : (022) 2385 6339 / 2386 9976, Fax : (022) 2386 9976
Email : niralimumbai@pragationline.com

☞ DISTRIBUTION BRANCHES

JALGAON

Nirali Prakashan   :   34, V. V. Golani Market, Navi Peth, Jalgaon 425001,
Maharashtra, Tel : (0257) 222 0395, Mob : 94234 91860

KOLHAPUR

Nirali Prakashan   :   New Mahadvar Road, Kedar Plaza, 1st Floor Opp. IDBI Bank
Kolhapur 416 012, Maharashtra. Mob : 9850046155

NAGPUR

Pratibha Book Distributors   :   Above Maratha Mandir, Shop No. 3, First Floor,
Rani Jhanshi Square, Sitabuldi, Nagpur 440012, Maharashtra
Tel : (0712) 254 7129

DELHI

Nirali Prakashan   :   4593/21, Basement, Aggarwal Lane 15, Ansari Road, Daryaganj
Near Times of India Building, New Delhi 110002
Mob : 08505972553

BENGALURU

Pragati Book House   :   House No. 1, Sanjeevappa Lane, Avenue Road Cross,
Opp. Rice Church, Bengaluru – 560002.
Tel : (080) 64513344, 64513355,Mob : 9880582331, 9845021552
Email:bharatsavla@yahoo.com

CHENNAI

Pragati Books   :   9/1, Montieth Road, Behind Taas Mahal, Egmore,
Chennai 600008 Tamil Nadu, Tel : (044) 6518 3535,
Mob : 94440 01782 / 98450 21552 / 98805 82331,
Email : bharatsavla@yahoo.com

niralipune@pragationline.com | www.pragationline.com

Also find us on 🅕 www.facebook.com/niralibooks

Preface to the First Edition...

We feel highly delighted in presenting this text book on "Labour Welfare" to the M.P.M. students preparing for their examination. The book has been written as per the syllabus prescribed for the M.P.M. Course, Part-I (Semester-II) and made effective from June, 2013.

Labour Welfare is very important from the view point of workers employed in different sectors and it deals with a variety of topics such as Labour Welfare, Labour Welfare Officer, Welfare Amenities, Maharashtra Workers' Welfare Board, etc. Considering the importance of Labour Welfare, all these topics are included in the syllabus by the University and have been explained in a simple manner in the book. Besides these topics, all the provisions of the Maharashtra Labour Welfare Fund Act of 1953 are also given. We hope that this book will help the students get acquainted with important aspects relating to labour welfare and will encourage them for further study. The students and other readers will find this book of immense use from the viewpoint of their examination.

In spite of sincere efforts, printing errors might have crept in the book at some places. We hope that we shall be excused for them.

We are very thankful to Shri Dineshbhai Furia, Shri Jignesh Furia our publishers and their team which includes, Mrs. Nirja Sharma, Prasad Chintakindi, Amit Kumar, Sarika Wagh, Ravindra Walodare, Mr. Parag Ghamandi and the entire staff of 'Nirali Prakashan', Pune for publishing the book.

We shall consider our labour amply rewarded if this book appreciated by those for whom it is meant.

We extend our good wishes to all students, teachers, and readers with the genuine hope that they will receive this book with great enthusiasm.

Pune   **Authors**
January 2014

Syllabus ...

UNIT 1

LABOUR WELFARE   [7 + 2]

Introduction and History, Definition, Scope, Objectives and Principles, Theories of labour welfare, ILO - & ILC Introduction and History, Scope, Objectives and Structure.

UNIT 2

LABOUR WELFARE OFFICER   [7 + 2]

Role, Qualifications, Functions, Duties of Labour Welfare Officer & Difference between Personnel Manager & Welfare Officer.

UNIT 3

WELFARE AMENITIES   [7 + 2]

Statutory Welfare Amenities. Government approaches & practices in Labour Welfare (Welfare & Health) in various sectors of Industry. Non-Statutory Welfare Amenities, Role of Trade Union, NGO's & Local Govt.

UNIT 4

WORKERS EDUCATION SCHEME AND WORKERS PARTICIPATION IN MANAGEMENT
                                                            [7 + 2]

Workers Education Scheme and Workers Participation in Management in Relation with Labour Welfare and Industrial Hygiene.   [6 + 2]

UNIT 5

MAHARASHTRA WORKERS WELFARE BOARD   [8 + 2]

The Bombay Labour Welfare Fund Act – 1953 • Social Security • Concepts and Components, Interrelationship of Welfare with Productivity, Relationship between Mental, Physical, Social and Industrial Health. Discussion of Two Cases (Problems) Related to Labour Welfare and Industrial Hygiene.

Contents ...

🖎🖎🖎

Chapter 1...

Labour Welfare

Contents ...

Learning Objectives

At the end of this chapter, you will understand :

- Meaning and definitions of 'Labour Welfare'
- Scope, objectives and principles of 'Labour Welfare'
- Various theories of Labour Welfare
- The objectives, structure, etc. of International Labour Organisation [ILO]

1.1 INTRODUCTION

'Labour' is one of the factors of production. Without the help of labour, production of goods and services is very difficult. Labour is one of the important factors of production which participates actively in the process of production. However, the process of production causes some adverse effects on physical and mental health and capacities of the workers and leads to fatigue. Therefore, care must be taken to reduce the adverse effects to the minimum. From this point of view, labour welfare is very important. Therefore, first let us try, to understand the meaning and nature of welfare.

'Welfare' means doing well. It is a comprehensive concept and refers to the physical, mental, moral and emotional well-being of the state of mind of an individual. Welfare cannot be seen as we see things around us, rather it can be experienced and enjoyed. Its effectiveness is very difficult to measure properly.

The other important aspect of welfare is that it is a concept relative to time and space. Therefore, it varies from time to time, from region to region, from person to person and from country to country.

Sometimes, welfare refers to a state of living of a person or a group of persons in a desirable relationship with total environment i.e. ecological, psychological, economic and social. Further, it also includes the social as well as economic contents of welfare.

In the study of labour work, we come across two concepts i.e. social welfare and economic welfare. Social welfare is primarily concerned with the solution of different problems of the people belonging to weaker sections of the society like prevention of destitution i.e. complete poverty. It aims at overall social development by means such as social legislation, social reform, social service, social action and work.

Economic welfare aims to promote economic development by increasing production and productivity, equitable distribution and satisfaction of economic wants of the people. Both, social as well as economic welfare, are important for labour welfare.

Labour welfare implies a state of well-being, happiness, development caused by social and economic welfare. In this chapter, we have to study the meaning and definitions of labour welfare, its principles objections, theories of labour welfare etc.

1.2 MEANING AND DEFINITIONS OF LABOUR WELFARE

Labour welfare implies providing various facilities such as proper lighting, heat control, cleanliness, low level of noise, toilet, spittoons, drinking water facilities, canteen, rest room facilities, various health and safety measures, all efforts to reduce and minimise worker's fatigue, various welfare services such as housing, education, recreations, transportation, counseling, etc. for improving the conditions of workers. The measures in the respect of the items mentioned above, if provided properly, add to improve social and economic conditions of workers and their families.

Labour welfare should be viewed as a total concept. The total concept implies a desirable state of existence which involves the physical, mental, moral and emotional well being. Labour welfare can be viewed as a social concept of welfare implying the welfare of workers, their facilities and the community in which they live. Further, the concept of labour welfare is flexible and elastic. It differs widely with time, person, region, industry, social values, customs, traditions, level of development and industrialisations, urbanisation, political ideologies in existence in a particular time. It also changes according to gender, marital, economic and social status, age-group, educational level of workers in different industries and regions. Because of all these factors, it is very difficult to define it precisely. However, attempts have been made to define it by the experts and organisations. Let us consider some such definitions of labour welfare.

(a) According to **E. S. Proud**, *"Welfare work is voluntary efforts on the part of employers to improve the existing industrial system and the conditions of employment in their own factories".*

(b) **R. R. Hopkins** stated that, *"Welfare is fundamentally an attitude of mind on the part of management, influencing the method by which management activities are undertaken".*

(c) According to **Arthur James Todd**, *"Welfare work is anything done for the comfort and improvement, intellectual and social of the employees over and above 'the wages paid, which is not a necessity of the industry".*

(d) In the **Encyclopedia of Social Sciences** the definition of labour welfare is given as *"The voluntary efforts of the employers to establish, within the existing industrial system, working and sometimes, living and cultural conditions of the employees beyond what is required by law, the custom of the country and the conditions of the market."*

(e) In its **Report the ILO** defined Labour Welfare as *"such services, facilities and amenities as adequate canteens, rest and recreation facilities, arrangements for travel to and from work and for the accommodation of workers employed at a distance from their houses, and such other services, amenities and facilities as contribute to improvements in the conditions under which workers are employed. "*

(f) According to the **Committee on Labour Welfare (1969)**, Labour Welfare includes *"such services, facilities and amenities as adequate canteens, rest and recreation facilities, sanitary and medical facilities, arrangements for travel to and from place of work, and for the accommodation of workers employed at a distance from their homes; and such other services, amenities and facilities , including social security measures, as contribute to the conditions under which workers are employed."*

(g) The **Labour Investigation Committee (1944-1945)** preferred to include under Labour Welfare : *"Anything done for the intellectual, physical, moral and economic betterment of the workers, whether by employers, by government or by other* *agencies, over and above what is laid down by law or what is normally expected of the contractual benefits for which workers may have bargained. "*

(h) **N. M. Joshi** made clear in his book, "Trade union movement in India" that, *"Labour welfare work covers all the efforts which employers make for the benefit of their employees over and above the minimum standards of working conditions fixed by the factories Act and over and above the provisions of the social legislations providing against accidents, old age, unemployment and sickness."*

Thus, labour welfare is important not only from the view point of workers, but it is important from the view point of economic and social development of a country.

From the definitions stated above, we come to know that the concept of labour welfare has been used in a 'wide' as well as 'narrow' sense. In the 'broader sense' it includes not only the minimum standard of hygiene and safety laid down in general labour legislation, but also such aspects of working life as social insurance schemes, measures for the protection of women and young workers, limitation of hours of work, paid vacations, etc. In the 'narrow sense', welfare in addition to general physical working conditions is mainly concerned with the day-to-day problem of the workers and of the social relationships at the place of work which leads to fatigue and affects adversely the efficiency and productivity of workers.

1.2.1 Characteristic Features of Labour Welfare Work

In simple words, labour welfare work includes all the efforts to make life worth living for workers and providing all such services and facilities for the better work conditions. They are known as statutory and nonstatutory labour welfare amenities provided by various agencies. From the definitions stated earlier, we can note down the important characteristic features of labour welfare work.

(a) Labour welfare work is the work which is undertaken within the premises of the establishments as well as outside the establishments for the benefit of employees and their family members.

(b) The main purpose of welfare amenities is to bring about the overall development of employees personality so that they become efficient, productive employees, good citizens and good member of their families.

(c) The labour welfare work basically includes all those services and facilities of labour welfare which are over and above what is expected by the employees as a result of a contract of service from their employers.

(d) It covers social security and various other activities as medical facilities, transfer facilities, recreational facilities etc.

(e) These facilities are provided by the employers at their own accord out of their realisation of social and moral responsibility towards workers or statutory provisions to make these facilities available to workers. They can also be provided by the government, trade unions and other voluntary associations.

(f) In the report of the committee on Labour Welfare 1969, it is stated that, "It may be noted that not only intra-mural but also extra-mural, statutory as well as non-statutory activities, undertaken by any of the three agencies the employers, trade unions or the government—for the physical and mental development of a worker, both as a compensation, for, wear and tear that he undergoes as a part of the production process and also to enable him to sustain and improve upon the basic capacity of contribution to the processes of production, "which are all the species of the longer family encompassed by the term 'Labour welfare."

The Committee of Experts on Welfare Facilities for Industrial Workers convened by ILO (in 1963) included the following items under the term, 'labour welfare."

Sr. No	Welfare Amenities within the Precincts of the Establishments	Welfare Facilities Outside the Establishment
1.	Latrines and urinals.	Maternity benefit.
2.	Washing and bathing facilities.	Social insurance measures (including gratuity, pension, provident fund and rehabilitation).
3.	Crèches.	Benevolent funds.
4.	Rest shelters and canteens.	Medical facilities (including programmes for physical fitness and efficiency, family planning and child welfare).
5.	Arrangements for drinking water.	Education facilities.
6.	Health services, including occupational safety.	Housing facilities.
7.	Arrangement for prevention of fatigue.	Recreation facilities (including sports, cultural activities, library, reading rooms).
8.	Administrative arrangements for the welfare of employees.	Holiday homes and leave travel facilities.
9.	Uniform and protective clothing.	Workers co-operatives, including consumers co-operatives stores, fair price shops, and cooperative credit and thrift societies.
10.	Shift allowance.	Vocational training for dependents of workers
		Other programmes for the welfare of women, youth and children.

1.3 NEED, AIMS AND OBJECTIVES OF LABOUR WELFARE

1.3.1 Need for Labour Welfare

The need for providing labour welfare facilities basically arises from the developing and rapidly changing industrial system which is characterised by two important factors. The first factor is that the conditions under which the workers work are not suitable and conducive for health and safety and the second factor is that a worker joins an establishment, he has to work in an entirely different atmosphere which creates problems of adjustment and the workers is disturbed thereby.

The working environment in establishments affects adversely the health of workers because of many factors, e.g. loud noise, excessive heat or cold, fumes and dust, lack of sanitation facilities, etc. These factors lead to occupational hazards. Hence, they are required to be prevented by necessary facilities, protective devices, etc. For these purposes, there is the need to provide necessary labour welfare facilities within the premises of factories, mines, plantations etc.

Labour welfare amenities are also needed for improving the efficiency and productivity of workers. The Labour Investigation committee pointed out that *the provision of canteens, medical aid, maternity and child welfare services improve the health of the workers and bring down the rates of general, maternal and infantile mortality; and education facilities increase their mental efficiency and economic productivity.*

The need for labour welfare is felt all the more in India because of the rapid development of industrial and other sectors which aim at rapid economic and social development.

The Royal Commission of Labour in 1931 pointed out that labour welfare work is needed because of the lack of commitment to industrial work among factory workers due to non-availability of sufficient, adequate welfare facilities and harsh treatment received from their employers. Considering these factors the need of labour welfare work has been emphasised by the constitution of India which contains the following important Articles in this respect.

Article 41: The state shall, within the limit of its economic capacity and development, make effective provisions for securing the right to work to education, and to public assistance in cases of unemployment, old-age, sickness, and disablement and in other cases of underserved want,"

Section 42: The state shall make provision for securing the just and humane conditions of work and for maternity relief."

Article 43: The state shall endeavour to secure, by suitable legislation or economic organisation, or in any other way, to all workers, agricultural, industrial or otherwise, work, a wage, conditions of work ensuring, a decent standard of life and full enjoyment of leisure and social and cultural opportunities; and in particular, the state shall endeavour to promote cottage industries on an individual or co-operative basis in rural areas."

Thus, it can be said that need for providing labour welfare amenities, facilities arises from the social responsibility of industry, a strong desire for upholding democratic values, concern of employees, for the improvement of working conditions and for the well-being of workers.

1.3.2 Aims of Labour Welfare

Industrial workers are soldiers and their actions and interactions in the industrial framework have a great impact and influence on industrial development. Economic development to a great extent depends on them. Therefore all sided efforts must be done for increasing labour welfare.

The aim of labour welfare activities or work is three-fold. It is partly humanistic since it enables the workers a richer life by making available to them; those amenities and conveniences of life which they themselves cannot provide. It is partly economic since it improves the efficiency and productivity of workers. Lastly, the aim is partly civil as it develops among the workers a sense of responsibility and dignity. Yet another aim of labour welfare is to help the workers to fulfill their future needs and aspirations. Thus, the ultimate aim of labour welfare is to make workers more happy and worthy citizens.

1.3.3 Objectives of Labour Welfare

It is considered that labour welfare has two aspects. On one hand, it is associated with the counteracting of the harmful effects of large-scale industrialisation on the personal, family and social life of the worker, while on the other hand, it deals with the provision of opportunities for the worker and his family for a socially and personally good life.'

In other words, labour welfare facilities counteract the handicaps to which the workers are exposed, both in their work-life and folk-life and they also provide opportunities and facilities for a harmonious development of overall personality of workers. Thus, it becomes clear that there are multiple objectives of labour welfare which are achieved through suitable labour welfare programmes.

Labour welfare has a humanitarian approach which has given way to a more practical utilitarian approach. This approach views that expenditure on labour welfare activities is an investment and its, gains are considerable in the form of increased efficiency and quicker and improved services from the employees. The important objectives of labour welfare are as follows :

(a)   To enhance efficiency and productivity of workers.

(b)   To motivate the workers to work hard, honestly and also to retain them i.e. to build stable work-force.

(c)   To develop loyalty in workers towards their organisations.

(d)   To develop better relations with employees.

(e)   To attract the best workers, employers offer certain welfare amenities.

(f)   To make life of workers worth living.

(g)   To make intellectual improvement and provide social comforts to employees.

(i)   To ensure higher standards of working conditions and keep atmosphere, healthy and pleasant at the work places.

(j)   To inculcate among the workers a sense of responsibility, dignity, belongingness etc.

(k)   To reduce absenteeism and labour turnover.

(l)   To fulfil the future needs and aspirations of the workers.

(m)   To help minimise social evils such as alcoholism, drug addiction. A worker is likely to fall victim to any of these evils if he is dissatisfied or frustrated. Welfare amenities tend to make the workers happy, cheerful and confident.

(n)   To create an atmosphere of goodwill between workers and the management and thereby to improve the image of the organisation in the society.

(o)   To provide good and healthy working and living conditions.

(p)   To ensure the well-being of the worker and their families.

(q)   To provide guidance wherever needed.

(r)   To provide counselling facilities to solve the problems of workers.

1.4 PRINCIPLES OF LABOUR WELFARE

For promoting labour welfare, various labour welfare schemes are launched and amenities, facilities, etc. are provided. But merely launching the schemes and making statutory provisions to provide welfare facilities, cannot be effective for progress of labour welfare. These schemes should be implemented and welfare facilities must be provided adequately. Hence, certain basic principles of labour welfare should be followed properly to achieve implementation of welfare schemes and programmes. These principles of labour welfare are explained below.

(a)   **Principle of Totality of Labour Welfare :** This principle considers labour welfare as a total concept. Labour welfare, according to this principle, must be spread throughout the hierarchy of an organisation and should not be restricted to any particular level. Labour welfare activities must be comprehensive enough to cover all the employees and the management should be welfare oriented at all levels and keen to implement various labour welfare programmes. Further all employees at all levels must accept the total concept of labour welfare positively. Otherwise, labour welfare programmes are not likely to be successful in the real sense.

(b)   **Principle of Integration and co-ordination :** There should be proper co-ordination, integration and also harmony of all labour welfare schemes, programmes and services in an organisation. A co-ordinated and integrated approach helps to promote proper healthy development and assures the success of labour welfare programmes.

(c) Principle of Responsibility : This principle plays an important role in the management of labour welfare programmes. There are many agencies, e.g. employers, trade unions, etc. involved in labour welfare management. Therefore, the responsibility must be shared by different groups to enhance labour welfare.

(d) Principle of Timeliness : If welfare services, amenities are provided whenever they are essential, they prove to be useful. Timeliness is essential in planning various labour programmes. Timely actions in proper direction is very essential in all kinds of welfare and social work.

(e) Principle of Accountability : This principle implies that there should be scientific periodical evaluation of welfare measures and timely improvements in the measures implemented and these should be evaluated on the basis of feedback. Therefore, this principle is also called as the principle of evaluation.

(f) Principle of Efficiency : This principle is based on the relationship between welfare and efficiency. Efficiency in rendering welfare services and providing welfare amenities ought to be there. Otherwise providing the amenities, services may not prove to be of adequate use. Both efficiency and welfare cannot be measured accurately and hence it is very difficult to measure the relationship between them.

(g) Principle of Re-personalisation : This principle considers the development of human personality as the goal of welfare. Hence, this principle should be practised to counteract the harmful effects on the industrial and social systems. For this purpose, it is very essential to render labour welfare services and to provide labour welfare amenities inside and outside the establishment.

(h) The Principle of Self-help : The principle of self-help should be followed even in our day to day life. Hence it is important in the sphere of labour welfare. The labour welfare must encourage the workers to help themselves, which makes them more responsible, productive, and efficient.

(i) Principle of Democratic Values : This principle emphasises the workers participation in respect of formulation and implementation of labour welfare schemes and programmes. Consideration of their opinions is essential for the success of the schemes and programmes. Industrial democracy is the driving force of this principle. If this principle is followed, the workers feel that they are worthy and thus will co-operate with the management in all respects.

(j) Principle of Adequacy of Wages : It should be noted that various welfare measures are not a substitute for wages or monetary incentive. The workers have the right to receive their wages in addition to the benefits of welfare measures.

(k) Principle of Social Responsibility of Industry : According to this principle, the industry or an organisation has obligations towards its workers in respect of providing welfare services and amenities. The organisation should consider it as a social obligation. Even the Constitution of India in its Directive Principle of State Policy emphasises this aspect of labour welfare.

The labour welfare work of an organisation should be administratively viable and must be development oriented.

1.5 HISTORY AND SCOPE OF LABOUR WELFARE

1.5.1 History of Labour Welfare

Along with development and progress of labour welfare activities, the scope of labour welfare is also widened. The study of historical development of labour welfare will help us understand the scope of labour welfare.

Labour welfare, as a movement began in the early year of Industrial Revolution especially in the western countries. The 21st century, witnessed the growth of labour welfare, to a great extent, due to the rapid growth of industrialisation, acceptance of modern techniques and changing social and political conditions.

The two World Wars gave considerable impetus to the labour welfare movement. Modern welfare is said to have been the outcome of the movement for better and more efficient management in industry including the human angle.

The origin of labour welfare activities in India can be traced to the First World War. The labour welfare activity was mainly influenced by the humanitarian principle and legislation in India. The conditions of labour were miserable. Exploitation, bad sanitation, long hours of work, exploitation, absence of safety measures, etc. were the regular features.

The British Government was not very keen in improving labour welfare. However, it introduced certain legislative measures for improving the conditions of working class. It started when the Apprentices Act of 1850 was passed. The next Act was the Fatal Accident Act of 1853. Then came the Merchants Shipping Act of 1959. The earlier attempts included at mainly legislation aiming at regulation of employment in India.

The movement for improving the conditions of workers started when the First Indian Factories Act was passed in 1881. But the conditions of workers did not improve. The Mulock Commission was appointed in 1884 by the Government to review the working of the Factories Act of 1881. Mr. N. M. Lokhande brought the workers together in 1884 and presented on the behalf of workers a charter of demands to the Mulock Commission. The Factries (Amendment) Act of 1891 was passed considering the recommendations of the Bombay factory 1884 and that of 1890. The Act made certain provisions with respect to working hours and sanitary conditions. However, there was no considerable progress in the field of labour welfare.

The establishment of ILO in 1919 was the important landmark in the history of labour welfare movement. Thereafter the first central trade union i.e. ATTUC was formed in India which helped the labour welfare movement to progress.

Following the industrial unrest during 1919-1920, the Government passed the Factories Act of 1922 which helped the conditions to improve with respect to working hours and conditions of welfare. Thereafter, in 1929, the Royal Commission of Labour was appointed to enquire the then existing conditions of workers, industrial undertakings, plantations, mines, etc. The Commission recommended the enactment of a number of legislations relating to payment of wage, working conditions, health insurance, etc. Many recommendations of the Commission were accepted with respect to labour welfare and there was improvement in conditions of work to some extent. Thereafter a number of Commissions and Committees were appointed for suggesting improvements in the condition of workers.

Another milestone in the labour welfare movement was the Labour Investigation Committee 1934. i.e. Rege Committee. The committee covered different areas in labour welfare such as sanitation, housing, medical aid, educational facilities, etc. The committee emphasised need for strengthening the enforcement machinery for effective implementation of legal provisions. ILO also supported the Indian labour welfare movement by suggesting various measures.

After 1947, the labour welfare movement grew and acquired new dimensions. The Government realised its social responsibility towards the weaker sections of the society and understood the importance of labour welfare. After 1947, many central unions were established, INTUC (1947), HMS (1949), UTUJ (1949), BMS (1955) CITU (1970) were a few among them which gave filip to the development of labour welfare movement.

The Constitution of India, began giving importance to labour welfare by passing many Labour Acts. The Factories Act of 1948, the Mines Act of 1952, the Plantations Labour Act of 1961, the Motor Transport Act of 1961, The Contract Labour Act of 1970, The Merchant Shipping Act of 1956 are some of the important Acts which provided various labour welfare facilities. The Government of India decided to march ahead by implementing five-year plans. In five year plans, considerable attention has been given to the welfare of working class.

In the last 63 years after the implementation of the First Five year plan, much has been done in the field of labour welfare. However, much is yet to be done to improve the conditions of working class.

1.5.2 Scope of Labour Welfare

The industrial field expands at a fast rate and there is considerable increase in the industrial activities. Various commissions and committees are appointed to study and to recommend what should be done to increase labour welfare. They recommend various measures for increasing labour welfare. Moreover, the labour class is encompassed of dynamic individuals with complex needs.

Therefore the field of study of labour welfare is expanding. Hence, It is difficult to lay down accurately the scope of labour welfare activities or work. However, the scope of labour welfare has been described by the experts in the field, various institutions and organisations engaged in labour welfare activities in different ways. Its scope is interpreted in different ways by different countries, with varying stages of economic development, political outlook and social philosophy.

Labour welfare work is generally considered to include everything done for the intellectual, moral, physical, social and economic betterment i.e. overall betterment of workers whether by the Government employees, trade union, workers organisations or by other agencies over and above what is laid down by legislations or what is normally expected as part of the contractual benefits for which the workers work or bargain.

The Committee of Experts on Welfare Facilities of International workers constituted by the ILO in 1963 divided the welfare amenities in two group i.e.

(1) Welfare amenities within the precincts of the establishment known as intra-mural amenities and

(2) Welfare amenities outside the establishment known as extra-mural amenities. These intro-mural and extra-mural amenities are covered in the scope of labour welfare studies.

The Encyclopedia of social sciences has made clear various labour welfare amenities by classifying them in the following three categories :

(I) All amenities or facilities dealing with immediate working conditions: These are special provisions for adequate light, heat, ventilation, toilet facilities, accident and occupational disease prevention, rest rooms lunchrooms, maximum hours, minimum wages, etc.

(II) All those amenities and facilities concerned with less immediate working conditions and group interest: These are gymnasiums, club rooms, playgrounds, gardens, dancing, music, mutual aid societies, vacation with pay, profit-sharing, stock ownership, disability and unemployment funds, pensions, saving banks provisions for conciliation and arbitration, shop committees and workers councils.

(III) All those amenities designed to improve community conditions: These include housing, retail stores, schools, libraries, kindergartens, lectures or domestic sciences, day nurseries, dispensary and dental service, screening of motion pictures, arranging athletic contest, picnic and summer camps, etc.

From the above list of welfare amenities and facilities provided to workers it can be concluded that labour welfare is a very flexible as well as comprehensive subject. It includes a multitude of activities of employees, trade unions, government which help the workers and their families in respect of their welfare.

1.6 THE THEORIES OF LABOUR WELFARE

The theories of labour welfare constitute the conceptual framework of labour welfare. There are about eight theories of labour welfare. These theories reflect the attitudes and approaches of different agencies which provide welfare amenities and services. Welfare amenities can be provided on religion, philanthropic, social or on other grounds. These different theories or approaches to labour welfare also reflect the evolution of the welfare concept.

In the past the government used to compel the employers to provide certain basic amenities such as canteen, drinking water, rest rooms, etc. to their employees. The compulsion was necessary because the employers were reluctant to provide the amenities to their employees and on the contrary they used to exploit the employees by treating them in an unfair manner.

However, time has changed and the welfare concept too has undergone changes. At present, it is found that many employers, establishments, trade unions and other social organisations provide various welfare facilities to their employees statutorily as well as willingly. This is indeed a noteworthy change.

Let us consider the theories of labour welfare.

(a) Policing Theory of Labour Welfare : It is undoubtedly true that at least a minimum standard of welfare is necessary for the workers to live. But the assumption of the theory is that the employers do not provide even the minimum welfare facilities to their workers without any compulsion. It is assumed in the theory that man is selfish and self-centered. He always tries to achieve his own objectives at the cost of the welfare of others. Hence, something must be done to protect the interest of workers in respect of labour welfare.

According to this policing theory, employers get opportunities to exploit workers and treat them in an unfair manner as the position of the employers is strong and that of their employees is weak. This could be done by asking the workers to work for long hours, by paying them low wages, by keeping work places in unhygienic conditions, by giving rude treatment, etc. But the government cannot remain merely a passive spectator of this limitless exploitation of workers. Hence, it has to intervene and compel the employers to provide at least minimum standard of welfare for the working class. For this purpose, many suitable Acts have been passed making the statutory provisions for providing certain welfare amenities to workers. Of course, such interference and intervention are in the interest of the progress and welfare of workers as well as that of economy. In short, this theory suggests that the government assumes the role of a policemen and compels the employers to provide statutory welfare facilities and punishes the non-compliers. It is also assumed in this theory that there should be periodical supervision to ascertain whether the welfare measures according to the provisions of the Acts applicable to labour welfare are provided and implemented or not.

(b) The Religious Theory of Labour Welfare : It is a well-known fact that man is a gregarious animal and also a religious one. Even in the modern era, many acts and actions of man are related to religious belief and sentiments. These feelings sometimes prompt the employers to take up some sort of welfare activities in the expectation of future emancipation either diring their life or even after it. Therefore, they consider welfare work as an investment for the present or for the future.

This theory has two important connotations, namely, the investment and atonement aspects. To atone means to make amends for an error or wrong. The investment aspect implies that the fruits of today's deeds or actions will be reaped in the future. Inspired by this belief, some employers provide various amenities to their employers e.g. canteen facilities, crèches, etc. The atonement aspect implies that the present disabilities of a person are the result of sins committed by him or her in the past. Hence he or she should undertake some good deeds to atone or compensate for the sins.

Of course, the religious basis underlying this theory does not seem to be rational. It is neither universal nor continuous. However, it is found that some employers provide certain labour welfare amenities for religious reasons.

(c) The Philanthropic Theory of Labour Welfare : 'Philanthropy' means love or affection for making or loving mankind. This word is derived from the Greek words 'Philos' and 'Anthropes'. Philos means loving while anthropes means man.

The philanthropic theory of labour welfare refers to the provisions of good working conditions, crèches, canteen, etc. out of love or pity on the parts of employers who wish to remove the disabilities of workers. Man is believed to have some sort of instinctive urge by which he makes sincere efforts to remove the suffering of other people and tries to promote their well-being. Perhaps, this drive can be more powerful and may impel him to perform noble sacrifices.

The labour welfare movement began in the early years of industrial revolution with the strong support of philanthropists. Sir Robert Owen of England was one of them and he worked for the welfare of workers.

This theory is more common in social welfare. However, its applicability is not universal and continuous. At the same time, it must be noted that the philanthropic sentiments on the part of employers and other concerned organisations have worked well in certain establishments and of course on certain occasions.

(d) Paternalistic Theory of Labour Welfare : This theory is also known as the trusteeship theory of labour welfare. According to this theory, the employer holds the total industrial estate, properties and assets, profit accruing from them in trust. He holds all the properties not for the use of himself but also for the benefits of his employees and also for the society. He plays the role of paternity or fatherhood. This theory implies that employers should provide necessary funds on an ongoing basis for the well-being of their employees for providing various amenities and helping to increase their welfare.

For several reasons, such as low wages, lack of education, etc. the employees are not able to take care of themselves. They are, like minors who cannot do much for their welfare on their own. Therefore, employers should provide various amenities for their well-being or welfare out of the funds in their control, of course, this trusteeship in not actual and legal, and hence not real. Hence labour welfare under this philosophy basically depends on the initiative of the employers. As it has no legal sanction, its effectiveness depends upon the moral conscience of the employers. Mahatma Gandhi, the father of our nation, strongly advocated this theory.

(e)   The Public Relation Theory of Labour Welfare : According to this theory, various welfare activities are provided to create a good impression on the workers and on the public in general. Thus, the theory provides a strong basis for an atmosphere of goodwill between the employer and his employees and also between employer and public.

As the employers provide certain amenities to their workers for creating a good impression, they utilise this for advertisement. As a result, sales are increased and industrial relations are also improved resulting in two fold benefit. When welfare programmes lose their advertisement value, the employers neglect programmes though they are useful for the welfare of the employees and welfare activities become a public stunt. This is a major drawback of this theory.

(f)   The Placating Theory of Labour Welfare : Placate means conciliate or to win the support of. This theory is based on the assumption that appeasement (i.e. soothing by giving what is wanted) pays when the workers are united and organised. Peace needed can be bought and brought by required welfare measures. Workers are like children who are intelligent but no so. As crying children are pacified or satisfied by sweets, ice-cream, etc. workers can be pleased if welfare amenities are provided to them. Thus, their support can be won. In short, this theory maintains that timely and periodical acts, of labour welfare can satisfy the workers and hence, certain amenities demanded by them should be provided.

(g)   The Functional Theory of Labour Welfare : This theory implies that welfare facilities are provided in order to make the workers more efficient. Therefore, this theory is also know as the efficiency theory of labour welfare. If workers are fed and nurtured properly, clothed adequately and treated kindly and further if their working conditions are congenial i.e. sympathetic, suitable, they work efficiently. Welfare work is the means of securing, preserving , increasing and maintaining the efficiency of workers. Thus, it is obvious that if an employer takes proper care of his workers, they become more efficient and productive.

Any higher production is beneficial to workers and their employer. Because of higher production, the workers get better wages and sometimes a share in profit, while the profit cf their employer increases. It is considered in this theory that higher production is possible through labour welfare measures.

(h)   Social Theory of Labour Welfare : Social aspect of labour welfare is also important besides other aspects. At present, social obligations of employers in the industrial sector is assuming great importance. This theory implies that a factor or any establishment is morally bound to make efforts to improve the conditions of the society in addition to the improvement of the conditions of working class. Labour welfare is gradually becoming social welfare.

1.7 ESTABLISHMENT OF THE INTERNATIONAL LABOUR ORGANISATION (ILO)

In the sphere of industrial development, the role of industrial revolution is immense. However, the industrial revolution which started in England in the 17th century and industrial progress made thereafter, has generated evil effects and a lot of inhuman conditions such as total discard of health and safety for the workers, their exploitation, slavery system of workers. The workers suffered most and had to live in miserable conditions. As a result, many thinkers, philanthropists advocated some sort of international action against the exploitation of workers and their miserable conditions. They demanded an enactment of international labour legislation for protecting the workers. They also advocated to set up some labour organisation for these purposes. Therefore, the International conference was held in Berlin in 1890 in which the representatives from fourteen countries attended the conference. In the conference various measures were suggested and adopted to improve working conditions without making any commitment.

Another conference was held at Brussels in 1897 in which a resolution was adopted for providing an international bureau for the protection of interests of labour. But the efforts of the Bureau did not materialise. Thereafter in 1900, a new International Association for Labour Legislation was set up, which was the fore-runner of the ILO. It is a result of the various efforts on the part of this Association, that a diplomatic conference was held in Berne in 1906 in order to study the adoption of this international conventions. One for reducing the poisonous substances in manufacturing processes and the other for regulating working hours for young people and women. However, the First World War broke in 1914 and no action was taken to adopt these two conventions.

After the end of the First World War in 1919, a peace conference was held in Paris, and the commission on International Labour Legislation was finally set up. The commission prepared a document which was incorporated in the peace treaty in the year 1919 called as 'Treaty of Versailles'. The Treaty emphasised the urgent need for regulation and protection of working the class involving the employees, employers, trade unions and government. It was also recommended to set up the international organisation for labour. As a result, the ILO was set up on 19th April, 1919 at Versailles.

The ILO symbolises social justice, universal peace and human dignity. It may be noted that India's policies and programmes in fulfilment of obligations towards the citizens of India, are also based on these three important concepts.

India became a member of the ILO as an original signatory to the treaty of peace in 1919.

The unique feature of the ILO is that, the representatives of management, government and labour participate in its proceedings. Its main objective is the improvement of labour conditions. When the United National Organisation (UNO) came into existence in 1946, the ILO became the first specialist agency of the UNO.

1.8 THE STRUCTURE OF THE ILO

The three principle organs or sub-systems of the ILO are as follows :

(a)   The International Labour Conference (ILC).

(b)   The Governing Body.

(c)   The International Labour Office.

The tripartite character of the ILO is the distinctive feature of the ILO as compared with other international organisations.

The ILC is the supreme deliberative body of the ILO. It is the supreme policy making and legislative body. The governing, body of the ILO is the executive council and International Labour office is the secretariat, operational headquarter and information centre. We shall consider the structure, functions, etc. of the ILC with the help of the International Labour office.

1.8.1 The Nature, Composition and Functions of the General Body

The General Body is one of the principal bodies of the ILO. It is a non-political and non-legislative tripartite body. It functions as the executive wing of the organisation. It carries out the decisions of the ILC with the help of the International Labour office.

It consists of the members representing governments, employers and workers. Some of the government member seats are not elective and are held by the States of chief industrial importance (Brazil, China, France, Germany, India, Italy, Japan, the Russian Federation, the United Kingdom and The United States). While remaining government members are appointed by the government delegates from the member states, attending the ILC in the election years. The members of the employers as well as that of workers are elected for a period of three years by the employers and workers delegations attending the conference in the same year.

Following are the important functions performed by the Governing Body of the ILO.

(1)   To co-ordinate the work of the ILO.

(2)   To make the appointment of the Director General of the office.

(3)   To scrutinise the budget.

(4)   To fix the dates, duration and agenda of the Regional Conference.

(5)   To decide the specific action to be taken on the resolutions adopted.

(6)   To draw an agenda for each session and subject to the decision of the international Labour Conference, decide what subject should be included in the agenda of the International Labour Conference.

(7)   To take follow up of the implementation by member states of the conventions and recommendations adopted by the conference.

The Governing Body of the ILO has the power to seek advisory opinions from the International Court of Justice with the consent of the International Labour conference.

1.8.2 The Nature and Functions of the International Labour Office

The International Labour office is the third major body in the ILO system. It functions as the secretariat of the ILO in Geneva. The Director General of the ILO is the chief executive of this office. He is appointed by the Governing Body and he acts as the Secretary General of the ILC. He is appointed for a period of ten years and his term of office can be extended by the Governing Body.

The staff of this office is appointed by the Director General. He is assisted by two deputy director generals, six director generals, one director of the International Institute for Labour studies, one director of the International Centre of Advanced Technical and Vocational Training, advisors, chiefs of division, and other staff from the member nations.

This office is a research body, a publishing house and a clearing house of information on problems relating to labour.

The constitution of the ILO describes the main functions of this office which are as follows:

(a) To prepare various documents on items of the agenda of the conference

(b) To assist governments in framing legislation on the basis of the decisions taken by the ILC.

(c) To perform function in connection with the observance of the conventions.

(d) To bring out publications dealing with industrial labour problems of international labour and social problems.

1.9 THE PRINCIPLES ON WHICH THE ILO WAS ORIGINALLY BASED

A conference was convened at Philadelphia in April 1944. As a result of these deliberations, the aims of the ILO were redefined. It was termed as the Declaration of Philadelphia and it was later on incorporated in the constitution of the ILO. The Philadelphia conferee reaffirmed the following principles of the ILO.

(1) Labour is not a commodity.

(2) Freedom of expression and of association is essential to sustain progress.

(3) Poverty any where constitutes a danger to prosperity everywhere.

(4) The war against want requires to be carried on with unrelenting vigour within each nation and by continuous and concerted international efforts in which the representatives of workers and employers enjoying equal status with those of governments join with them in free discussion and democratic decision for the promotion of common welfare. It also asserts the primacy of the social objective in international policy i.e., the attainment of conditions in which all human being irrespective of race, creed or gender, have the right to pursue both their material well-being and their spiritual development in conditions of freedom and dignity, of economic security and equal opportunity.

1.10 THE OBJECTIVES OF THE ILO

The objectives of the ILO have been enunciated in the preamble to its constitution supplemented by the Article No. 427 of the peace Treaty of Versailles, 1919 and also by the Philadelphia Declaration of 1944.

The ideology of the ILO has been defined by instruments in the following terms.

"Whereas universal and lasting peace can be established only if it is based upon social justice."

And whereas such conditions of labour exists involving injustice, hardship and privation to large number of people as to produce unrest so great that the peace and harmony of the world are imperiled to unrest.

And whereas also the failure of any nation to adopt human conditions of labour is an obstacle in the way of other nations which desire to improve the conditions in their own countries and its citizens.

Thus the International Labour Organisation has been attempting to promote world - wide respect for the freedom and the dignity of the working men and to create the conditions in which that freedom and dignity can be fully and effectively enjoyed.

The Declaration of Philadelphia set forth ten objectives which the ILO was to further promote among all nations of the world. The theme underlying these objectives is social justice. These are as follows :

(1) Full employment and the raising of standard of living.

(2) The employment of workers in the occupations in which they can have the satisfaction of giving the fullest measure of their skill and attainments and make their greatest contribution to the common well-being.

(3) The provision, as a means to the attainment of this end, and under adequate guarantees for all concerned, of facilities for training and the transfer of labour, including migration for employment and settlement.

(4) Policies in regard to wages and earnings, hours and other conditions of work calculated to ensure a fair share of the fruits of progress to all, and a minimum living wage to all employed and in need of such protection.

(5) The effective recognition of right of collective bargaining, the co-operation of management and labour in the continuous improvement of productive efficiency, and labour in the continuous improvement of productive efficiency, and the collaboration of workers and employers in the preparation and application of social and economic measures.

(6) The extension of social security measures to provide a basic income to all in need of such protection and comprehensive medical care.

(7) Adequate protection for the life and health of worker in all occupations.

(8) Provision for child welfare and maternity protection.

(9) The provision of adequate nutrition, housing facilities for recreation and culture.

(10) The assurance of equality of educational and vocational opportunity.

1.11 THE FUNCTIONS AND SCOPE OF THE ILO

The influence of ILO on the labour policy and labour legislation in almost all progressive countries cannot be denied. As a matter of fact, labour and labour legislation of these countries are generally based on the principles enunciated and the provisions laid down in the International Labour Code of the ILO. The ILO undertakes many activities and performs various functions for overall development of the working class. Therefore, its scope is very vast which can be understood from the functions it performs and the activities which have been undertaken by it.

The important functions of the ILO are to remove the hardships and privations of the to ling masses all over the world and to ensure economic justice for them. Further it does all the efforts to improve the living standards of the working class and working conditions and thereby establishing a universal and lasting peace based on social justice.

Besides the above mentioned two functions or activities, the ILO works in the following areas.

(a) A major part of the work and activities consists of providing expert advice and technical assistance to its member states. Many activities lie in different fields like training, social security, occupational health and safety, workers education, industrial relations, etc. These areas in which the ILO works are very vast and hence, the scope or working, functioning of the ILO is vast and expanding too.

(b) To frame and launch the programmes on manpower development and vocational training. The ILO makes available manpower experts especially to developing countries for assessing their manpower needs and for organising vocational training programmes. The ILO is also involved in the area of productivity and management development programmes.

(c) To make all the efforts to promote equality for migrant workers in all social economic and labour matters.

(d) The constitution to the ILO specifically provides for the protection of women workers. It aims in regard to women workers :

   (i) Opportunities to provide educational facilities for their development.

   (ii) To prove full guarantee of civil and political rights.

   (iii) To make all efforts for equal pay for equal work.

   (iv) To provide legal protection against dangerous working conditions.

   (v) To protect women from economic exploitation.

(e) The work of ILO in the field of social security is pioneering. Many conventions deal with workmen's compensation, sickness and diseases, old age and survivor's insurance, unemployment provisions, maternity provisions. The functions of the ILO so far in these aspects are very important.

(f) To deal with the problems of child workers is an important function of the ILO. It has played a very significant role in the fight against the exploitation of children by setting standards, regulating the minimum age for admission of work, the recruitment of children into unhealthy and dangerous jobs. Protection of children workers is one of the important functions of the ILO.

(g) The ILO has paid considerable attention to the conditions of work of labour, hours of work, holidays with pay, principles and methods of wage regulations, etc.

The above mentioned functions of the ILO are noteworthy. However, the list of functions performed by the ILO is not complete. It is very difficult to enumerate all the functions of the ILO because of their vast nature.

1.12 THE NATURE, STRUCTURE AND FUNCTIONS OF THE INTERNATIONAL LABOUR CONFERENCE [ILC]

The ILC is a very important body of the ILO and it participates in policy making. The ILC comprises four main groups representing the government, employers and workers in the ratio 2 : 1 : 1. The session of the ILC are held at least once a year and all delegates are allowed to be accompanied by advisors not more than two for each item on the agenda.

The government delegates are mostly ministers, diplomats or officials. Employers and Workers' delegates are nominated by the government consulting the relevant industrial organisations according to the provision made in the constitution of the ILO.

There are seven committees of the ILC which are mentioned below :

(1) The Selection Committee
(2) The Credential Committee
(3) The Resolution Committee
(4) The Committee for the Application of Conventions and Recommendations
(5) The Drafting Committee
(6) The Committee on Standing Orders
(7) The Finance Committee

The ILC examines various social problems and adopts conventions and recommendations for ratification by governments. The ILC has adopted more than 300 conventions on a variety of subjects.

The ILC discussed the issue of equal pay in 1950-51 and in 1952 adopted a convention (i.e. formal agreement) by 105 votes to 33 and a recommendation by 146 votes to 18. Thus, the convention was made.

The ILC is the supreme organ of the ILO and it acts as the legislative wing of the ILO. Many times, special sessions of the ILC are also convened to deal with important questions relating to maritime labour. The ILC performs many functions. Important functions are mentioned below :

(1) To select once in 3 years members of the Governing Body.

(2) To elect its Presidents.

(3) To seek advisory opinion from the international committee of justice.

(4) To confirm the powers, functions and procedures of Regional conference.

(5) To formulate Labour Standards.

(6) To fix the amount of contributions by the member states.

(7) To decide the expenditure budget estimates prepared by the Director General and submit to the Governing Body.

(8) To make amendments to the constitution subject to subsequent ratification of the amendments by the 2/3 member states including 5 of the 10 states of industrial importance.

(9) To consider the report, of the Director General giving labour problems and assists in their solution.

(10) To appoint committees to deal with different matters during each session.

(11) To provide a forum for discussing the labour and social issues.

(12) To adopt amendments whenever done to the constitution.

The ILC is empowered to regulate its own procedures for carrying out its business.

POINTS TO REMEMBER

1. Characteristic Features of Labour Welfare Work

(a) Labour welfare work is the work which is undertaken within the premises of the establishments as well as outside the establishments for the benefit of employees and their family members.

(b) The main purpose of welfare amenities is to bring about the overall development of employees personality so that they become efficient, productive employees, good citizens and good member of their families.

(c) The labour welfare work basically include all those services and facilities of labour welfare which are over and above what is expected by the employees as a result of a contract of service from their employers.

(d) It covers social security and various other activities as medical facilities, transfer facilities, recreational facilities etc.

(e) These facilities are provided by the employers at their own accord out of their realisation of social and moral responsibility towards workers or statutory provisions to make these facilities available to workers. They can also be provided by the government, trade unions and other voluntary associations.

2. Principles of Labour Welfare

(a) Principle of Totality of Labour Welfare

(b) Principle of Integration and co-ordination

(c) Principle of Responsibility

(d) Principle of Timeliness

(e) Principle of Accountability

(f) Principle of Efficiency

(g) Principle of Re-personalisation

(h) The Principle of Self-help

(i) Principle of Democratic Values

(j) Principle of Adequacy of Wages

(k) Principle of Social Responsibility of Industry

3. The Theories of Labour Welfare

(a) Policing Theory of Labour Welfare

(b) The Religious Theory of Labour Welfare

(c) The Philanthropic Theory of Labour Welfare

(d) Paternalistic Theory of Labour Welfare

(e) The Public Relation Theory of Labour Welfare

(f) The Placating Theory of Labour Welfare

(g) The Functional Theory of Labour Welfare

(h) Social Theory of Labour Welfare

QUESTIONS FOR DISCUSSION

Q.1   Explain the meaning and objectives of 'Labour Welfare'.

Q.2   What is meant by 'Labour Welfare'? State its principles.

Q.3   Explain the meaning and scope of labour welfare.

Q.4   Explain Policing Theory and Religious Theory of labour welfare.

Q.5   State and explain the Philanthropic Theory of labour welfare.

Q.6   Explain the function, theory of labour welfare and make clear its importance.

Q.7   Explain the structure and objectives of the ILO.

Q.8   State the objectives and functions of the ILO.

Q.9   Explain the nature, structure and functions of the ILC.

Q.10   Write short notes on the following :

       (a)   Meaning and scope of 'Labour welfare'.

       (b)   Objectives and Principle of 'Labour welfare'.

       (c)   Theories of Labour welfare.

       (d)   Objectives and structure of the ILO.

       (e)   Objective and functions of the ILO.

       (f)   The functions of the ILC.

       (g)   The ILO and the ILC.

QUESTIONS FROM PREVIOUS EXAMINATIONS

Q.1   Describe the various theories of Labour Welfare.   [April-2013]

Q.2   Explain the different objectives of Labour Welfare.   [April-2013]

Q.3   Define the term 'Labour Welfare' and describe the various theories of Labour Welfare.   [Dec-2012]

Q.4   Explain the objectives of Labour Welfare.   [Dec-2012]

Q.5   Define Labour Welfare with its Scope and Objectives.   [April-2006]

Q.6   Explain the term Labour Welfare. Discuss the Theories of Labour Welfare.

                                                              [April-2007]

Q.7   What is the Scope of Labour Welfare? State its Principles.   [Dec-2007]

Q.8   Define the term 'Labour Welfare'. Describe the Various Principles of Labour Welfare.   [April-2010]

Q.9   Define Labour Welfare. Describe the Principles of Labour Welfare.   [April-2009]

Q.10   Explain the concept of 'Labour Welfare'. State Philosophy, Principles and Goals of Labour Welfare.   [Dec-2010]

Q.11   Explain the Scope and Objectives of Labour Welfare.   [April-2011]

Q.12   Write Short Notes on :

       (a)   Objectives of ILO.   [Dec-2010]

       (b)   Police Theory of Labour Welfare.   [April-2009]

Q.13   Bring out the Scope of Labour Welfare.   [April-2009]

Q.14   Explain the Objectives and Structure of ILO and Describe the Role of ILO in Promoting the welfare of the Labour.   [April-2010, 2011]

☞   ☞   ☞

Chapter **2**...

Labour Welfare Officer

Contents ...

Learning Objectives

At the end of the chapter, you will understand :

- How the welfare officers are appointed
- The qualifications of welfare officers
- Functions and duties of welfare officers
- Role of welfare officers
- Difference between personnel manager and labour welfare officer

---

2.1 INTRODUCTION

A Labour Officer is a Liaison Officer between the management and labour whose main responsibilities are :

(1)   To maintain a harmonious relationship between the factory management and workers.

(2)   To bring to the notice of management, grievances of workers.

(3)   To help management formulate labour policies and interpret them to the workers.

The Royal Commission on Labour in India, 1931 in its report strongly recommended the appointment of labour officers to protect the workers from jobbery and indebtedness and also to act as spokesmen of labour and protect amicable relations between workers and management. Thus, this position of Labour Welfare Officers owes its origin to the recommendations of the Royal Commission on Labour.

The commission made it clear that the jobbers should not be permitted to engage and dismiss the labour and this could be achieved by appointing labour welfare officers in all the factories. It was also made clear by the commission that the labour welfare officer should ensure that no employee is discharged without adequate causes. The commission also suggested certain duties which should be performed by the labour welfare officer, particularly in respect of welfare of the labour. Thus, the post of the labour officer was initially instituted to :

(a)   Develop and improve labour administration.

(b)   Eliminate the evils and malpractices of the jobber system in the recruitment of labour.

(c)   Serve as a liaison with the State Labour Commissioner.

In 1931, the Bombay Mill Owners' appointed labour officers on their own for settling disputes and grievances. Under the directions of the Jute Mills' Association, similar officers were appointed with certain duties in the Jute industry in Bengal. In spite of the recommendations of the commission, nothing substantial was done and the employers continued to prefer to retain the services of the jobbers. But when popular ministries were installed in 1937 in some of the states in India, they forced the employers to appoint and employ full-time functionaries - labour officers in their factories.

During the period of the Second World War, the labour officers were entrusted with the handling of labour administration and welfare activities. The functions of the labour officers were enlarged by the social reform movement in India, in wake of the public pressure for improving administration and growth of modern management movement in Indian industries. The functions of labour officers thereafter included various functions relating to welfare, personnel as well as industrial relations. Moreover, labour officers began to be designated as Labour Welfare Officers'.

The growth of industries necessitated increased welfare measures which the state could not always provide. Many benevolent employers took the initiative and appointed doctors and nurses to look after workers health and provided crèches facilities for the children of women employees. Calico Mills was one which provided these facilities in 1915. Miss Anusuya Sarabhai and Mr. Bankar initiated a network of labour welfare activities in 1917 which were taken over by the Textile Labour Association later. By 1920-21, several mills appointed labour welfare officers.

The labour welfare officers initially played the role of the social workers and recruitment officers to free workers from the clutches of jobbers, who used to make money at the cost of illiterate workers in different ways. Later on, it was made a statutory requirement. Here is the legislative provision for the appointment of welfare officers in the Factories Act of 1948. The Act was first conceived in 1881 to provide safety measures for the workers and thereafter amended from time to time.

However, the Act when implemented revealed many defects and weaknesses which hampered effective administration of the Act. Further, the provisions of the Act regarding safety, health and welfare of workers were also found to be inadequate and unsatisfactory. It was, therefore, felt that in view of large and growing industrial activities, a radical overhauling of the law relating to factories was necessary and hence the Factories Act of 1948 was passed in which we find the provisions of the appointment of welfare officers.

2.2 APPOINTMENT AND QUALIFICATIONS OF LABOUR WELFARE OFFICER

There is a legislative provision for appointing the welfare officers in the Factories Act of 1948. **Section 49 (1)** expressly provides for the appointment of welfare officers. It is stated in Section 49 (1) that, *"In every factory wherein five hundred or more workers are ordinarily employed the occupier shall employ in the factory such number of welfare officers as may be prescribed'*. This implies that there must be at least one welfare officer appointment as per prescribed qualifications and conditions of service. However, if the number of workers is more than two thousand five hundred, assistant or/and additional welfare officers are required to be appointed to assist the welfare officer. Table 2.1 shows, the number of welfare officers, assistance or additional welfare officers required to be appointed for a given number of workers.

Table 2.1 : Requirement of Number of Welfare Officers, Assistant or Additional Welfare Officers

Sr. No.	Where the number of workers exceeds	But does not exceed	No. of assistant or additional welfare officers
1.	500	2,500	One Welfare Officer.
2.	2,500	3,500	One Assistant Welfare Officer.
3.	3,500	4,500	One Additional Welfare Officer.
4.	4,500	6,500	One Additional and One Assistant Welfare Officer.
5.	6,500	8,500	Two Additional Welfare Officers.
6.	8,500	10,500	Two Additional Welfare Officers and One Assistant Welfare Officer.
7.	10,500	Above 10,500	Three Additional Welfare Officers.

It may be noted that even if a factory employs more than five hundred workers for a few months in the year and not continuously, the occupier has to employ the prescribed number of welfare officers. It was held in Employees' Association of Northern India Verses Secretary of Labour case [A.I.R. (1952) All.109] that the provisions of Section 49 (1) are applicable to those sugar factories also wherein five hundred or more workers are employed even for a few months in a year.

In the Mines Act of 1952, a provision to appoint welfare officers is made. It is stated in **Section 58 (9)** that, "*For requiring employment in every mine wherein five hundred or more persons are ordinarily employed, of such number of welfare officers as may be specified and for prescribing the qualifications and the terms and conditions of, and the duties to be performed by such welfare officers*".

In the Plantations Labour Act of 1951, there is also a provision to appoint welfare officers. Accordingly, every plantation wherein three hundred or more persons are ordinarily employed, the employer has to employ such number of welfare officers as prescribed.

2.2.1 Qualifications of Labour Welfare Officer

The rules framed by most of the States in India require a Labour Welfare Officer to have a minimum qualification of Master's Degree, or an equivalent diploma from a recognised institute/university with the knowledge of the local language.

In **Section 49 (2)** of the Factories Act, it is made clear that "*the State Government may prescribe the duties, qualifications and conditions of service of welfare officers*'.

After going through the views expressed by the State Governments, public sector undertakings, private employers' organisations, workers' organisations, experts in the field of industrial relations, the committee on Labour Welfare (1969) recommended that the management should designate one of the existing officers to the personnel department as 'Welfare Officer' to fulfil the purpose of the law. The management should ensure that only such officers of the personnel department are designated to look after the welfare activities as are properly qualified to hold these posts and have aptitude for welfare work".

A welfare officer to be appointed should possess the following qualifications :

(a)   A University degree or a Master's degree.

(b)   Degree or diploma in social sciences, social work or social welfare from any recognised institution/university.

(c)   An adequate knowledge of the language spoken by the majority of the workers in the area where the factories, mills and plantations are situated.

2.2.2 Appointment and Qualifications of 'Welfare Officer' According to the Maharashtra Welfare Officers (Duties, Qualifications and Conditions of Service) Rules of 1966

In exercise of the powers conferred by Section 112 read with Section 49 of the Factories Act of 1948, the Government of Maharashtra has made the Rules called as the Maharashtra Welfare Officers (duties, qualifications and conditions of service) Rules of 1966. These rules extend to the whole State of Maharashtra.

According to Rule 3 of the M.W.O. (duties, qualifications and conditions of service) Rules of 1966, a person is not eligible for the appointment as a Welfare Officer, Additional Welfare Officer or Assistant Welfare Officer unless he :

(a)   Has obtained a degree or diploma in social science recognised by the State Government in this behalf, has qualified at a viva voce test conducted by the Chief Inspector of the Factories, Mumbai as provided. This test consists of a test of general knowledge and in particular of labour problems pertaining to the Maharashtra state.

(b)   Has adequate knowledge of Marathi language.

(c)   No person who is directly or indirectly interested in any factory or in any patent or machinery connected with it shall be appointed as the Welfare Officer, the Additional Welfare Officer or Assistant Welfare Officer and he shall be allowed to hold such office after he becomes so interested in the factory.

It is also mentioned in the Rules that the posts of the welfare officers are to be filled in by an advertisement in at least two newspapers circulating in the region in which the factory is situated and out of which one must be in English Language. The selection must be made by the committee appointed by the employer and the appointment must be notified to the Chief Inspector of the Factories giving full details of the qualifications of the persons appointment.

2.3 FUNCTIONS AND DUTIES OF A LABOUR WELFARE OFFICER

2.3.1 Functions of a Labour Welfare Officer

The labour welfare officer performs a variety of functions such as supervising the provisions of welfare amenities in respect of the law and in matters of safety, health, housing, recreation facilities, various sanitary services, grant of leave with wages, welfare facilities as provided in the Factories Act, etc.

The welfare officers act as a counsellor in personal matters and any other problems of adjustment, rights and privileges. Further, they assist their management in formulating labour and welfare policies, development of fringe benefits, conducting workers' education and training programmes.

The welfare officers help departmental heads to meet their obligations under various Acts. They are a liaison between the establishment and outside agencies such as factory inspectors, medical officers etc. and help in the enforcement of various Acts relating to workers' welfare. They also help the workers to make better use of community services.

The care of workers in all matters affecting their well-being, both at the place of work and outside, puts a special responsibility on the welfare officers. From this point of view, they have to perform various functions as asked by their management. They function mainly as staff-advisor or specialist. They are expected to act as advisers, counsellors, mediators and also liaison-men between their managements and labour. In short, the functions entrusted to welfare officer's range from assisting the management in policy formulation and implementation to supervising welfare programmes, establishing the contacts with workers and public, solving workers' problems and grievances. Thus, they are multi-purpose personnel officers.

Considering the nature of the work of the welfare officers, their functions can be classified into three major categories :

(a)   Labour Welfare Functions.

(b)   Labour Administration Functions.

(c)   Labour Relations Functions.

Labour welfare functions mainly include labour welfare advice and assistance in implementing legislative as well as non-legislative provisions relating to the following matters or aspects :

(a)   Health and safety measures.

(b)   Sanitation and cleanliness.

(c)   Welfare amenities.

(d)   Working conditions.

(e)   Recreation of workers.

(f)   Various services like housing, provision of grains, other commodities etc.

(g)   Formation of welfare committees.

(h)   Lighting facilities.

i)   Implementation of Welfare Acts.

Labour administration functions of welfare officers are also important. These functions cover the following :

(i)   Safety and medical administration.

(ii)   Overall organisational discipline so far as workers are concerned.

(iii)   Wage and salary administration.

(iv)   Administration of legislation covering industrial relations.

Labour relations functions are very important from the point of view of smooth working of the organisation or enterprise. Labour relations means the relations which exist between employer and employees. Good labour relations help to protect and safeguard the interests of the employers and labour.

A large number of labour legislations have been enacted to promote the conditions of the workers e.g. The Factories Act of 1948, The Employees' State Insurance Act of 1948, the Workmen's Compensation Act of 1923 etc. The labour relation functions include mainly the following functions :

(a)   Settlement of grievances.

(b)   Settlement of labour disputes.

(c)   Various steps to be taken for increasing the productive efficiency of labour.

(d)   Administration of standing orders.

(e)   Proper management of the trade unions.

2.3.2 Duties of a Labour Welfare Officer

The duties of a Labour Welfare Officer are essentially supervisory. Since he is appointed by the management and is paid by the management, he is dependent on them for many things e.g. promotions, pay, various facilities and allowances etc. Therefore, he has to perform various duties which he has been asked to perform. The Central Model Rules, 1957 (Rule 7) make clear the duties of welfare officers very widely.

The Committee on Labour Welfare also detailed out various duties of labour welfare officers based on the model rules framed under the Factories Act of 1948. Let us first consider the duties of welfare officers as given in the Central Model Rules of 1957. Accordingly, the important duties of the labour welfare officers include the following :

(a)   To help and maintain harmonious relations between management and workers.

(b)   Redressal of workers' grievances.

(c)   To watch industrial relations and to settle disputes by persuasive efforts.

(d)   To provide feedback to management regarding labour's point of view to shape and formulate necessary labour policies and also to interpret these policies to the workers.

(e)   To advice management on the implementation of health and safety programmes for the welfare of labour.

(f)   To introduce and implement various measures for promoting productive efficiency of labour.

(g)   To make better the working conditions of workers.

(h)   To help the workers to adjust and adapt themselves to working environment.

(i)   Personnel counselling and advising workers on their individual personal problems.

Now, let us consider the duties of labour welfare officers based on the model rules framed under the Factories Act of 1948 as detailed out by the Committee on Labour Welfare. They are as follows :

(a) Supervision of :
1. Safety, health and welfare programmes like housing, recreation, sanitation services as provided under the law or otherwise.
2. Working of joint committees.
3. Grant of leave with wages according to the provisions and rules of the related Acts.
4. Redressal of the grievances of workers.

(b) Advising the management in respect of the following matters :
1. Formulation of labour and welfare policies.
2. Meeting the statutory obligations relating to workers.
3. Apprenticeship training programmes.
4. Developing proper and suitable fringe benefits programmes.
5. Workers' education programmes.

(c) Counselling the workers in the following matters :
1. Personnel and family problems.
2. Adjustment to their work environment.
3. Understanding their rights, duties and privileges.

(d) Establishing liaison with workers so that they may :
1. Understand the limitations under which they have to work.
2. Appreciate the need for harmonious and smooth industrial relations at the places where they work.
3. Understand and interpret company/organisation's policies properly.
4. Come to a settlement of disputes amicably.

(e) Liaisoning with management so that the management may :
1. Appreciate the workers' viewpoint on organisational matters.
2. Allow the welfare officers to intervene on behalf of workers in various matters under the consideration of the management.
3. Help departmental heads to meet their obligations and responsibilities under the Act.
4. Arrange for prompt redressal of various grievances of labour and speedy settlement of industrial disputes and maintain harmonious industrial relations in the organisation.
5. Introduce various measures for the well-being of workers.
6. Introduce measures to increase the productivity and efficiency of workers.

(f) Working with outside public and agencies so that :

1. A proper enforcement of various Acts as applicable to the plant/factories by establishing contact with the factory inspectors, medical officers etc. may be effectively achieved.

2. Various other agencies in the community may be assisted to help the workers to make use of community services.

From the duties of the welfare officers mentioned above, we come to know that the special responsibility is put on the labour welfare officers to take care of the workers in various matters affecting the well-being of workers at the place of work and outside for increasing the welfare of working class. Therefore, these officers can be considered as maintenance engineers on the human side.

2.3.3 Duties of a Labour Welfare Officer as given in the Maharashtra Welfare Officer Rules of 1966

In exercise of powers conferred by Section 49 (2), Section 50 and Section 112 of the Factories Act of 1948, the government of Maharashtra has made certain rules regarding the duties of welfare officers, additional welfare officers and assistant welfare officers. These rules have been included in Rule 7 of the M.W.O. rules of 1966. While Rule 7A makes it clear under the heading 'Non-performance of other duties', the duties or work not be performed by these officers.

According to Rule 7, following are the duties of a Labour Welfare Officer :

(a) To establish contacts and hold consultations with a view to maintaining harmonious relations between the factory management and workers.

(b) To bring to the notice of the factory management the grievances of workers, individual as well as collective, with a view to securing their expeditious redressal.

(c) To study and understand the point of view of labour in order to help the factory management to shape and formulate labour policies and interpret these policies to the workers in a language they can understand.

(d) To watch industrial relations with a view to using his influence to prevent a dispute arising between the factory management and workers, and in the event of a dispute having arisen, to help to bring about a settlement by persuasive efforts.

(e) To advise workers resorting to illegal strikes and the management against declaring illegal lockouts and to help in preventing anti-social activities.

(f) To maintain an impartial attitude during legal strikes or lockouts and to help bring about a peaceful settlement.

(g) To advise and assist the factory management in the fulfilment of various obligations, statutory or otherwise. To establish liaison with the Factory Inspector and the Medical Service concerning medical examinations of employees, health records, supervision of hazardous job; to visit workers when they are sick and convalescing; to take steps for the prevention of accidents; to supervise the functioning of the safety committee; to supervise plant inspection, safety education, investigation of accidents, maternity benefits and workmen's compensation.

(h) To promote relations between factory management and workers which will ensure productive efficiency as well as amelioration in their working conditions and to help workers to adjust and adapt themselves to their work environments.

(i) To encourage the formation of works and joint production committees, co-operative societies, safety first and welfare committees, and to supervise their work.

(J) To advise on, and assist factory management in the provision of amenities, such as canteens, shelters for rest, crèches, adequate latrine facilities, drinking water facilities, sickness and benevolent payments, pension and superannuation funds, and gratuity payments.

(k) To help the factory management in regulating the grant of leave with wages and explain to the workers the provisions relating to leave with wages and other leave privileges, and to guide them in matters of submission of applications for the grant of leave, and for regulating unauthorised absence.

(l) To advise on, and assist factory management in, providing welfare facilities such as housing facilities, foodstuffs, social and recreational facilities, sanitation, education of children and advice on individual personal problems.

(m) To advise the factory management on questions relating to the training of new starters apprentices, workers on transfer and promotion, instruction and supervisors, supervision and control of notice board and information bulletins for further education of workers and to encourage their attendance at technical institutes.

(n) To suggest measures to raise the standard of living of workers and in general promote their well-being

(o) To bring to the notice of workers their rights and liabilities under the Standing Orders of the factory and other rules which grant rights to, define the duties of, workers, or which are directed to the discipline, safety and protection of workers and the factory.

2.3.4 Rules 7A : Non-performance of Other Duties

If the Chief Inspector of Factories, Bombay, is of the opinion that a Welfare Officer, Additional Welfare Officer, or an Assistant Welfare Officer is being required or permitted by his employer to do work which is inconsistent with or detrimental to the performance of his duties prescribed by Rule 7, the Chief Inspector of Factories may, by an order in writing, direct that such Welfare Officer, Additional Welfare Officer, or Assistant Welfare Officer, as the case may be, shall not be required or permitted to do such work.

2.4 ROLE OF LABOUR WELFARE OFFICER

Labour welfare is an important facet of industrial relations, the extra dimension, giving satisfaction to the worker in a way even a good wage cannot. With the growth of industrialisation, economic development, labour welfare has definitely acquired added importance. All the workers working in different sectors cannot cope with the pace of modern life with minimum sustenance amenities. They need an added stimulus to keep their body and soul together. Though employers have realised the importance of their role in providing various extra amenities, welfare facilities, are not always able to fulfil workers' demand however reasonable they might be. They are primarily concerned with the viability and development of their organisations. Though labour welfare has been proved to contribute to efficiency in production, it is expensive.

Generally, it is found that an employer gives varying degrees of importance to labour welfare depending on his priorities. Therefore, the government knows it very well that all employers are not progressive minded and they may hesitate to provide even basis welfare measures. Hence, it introduces statutory legislation to bring about some measure of uniformity in certain amenities available to labour. The Committee on Labour Welfare (C.L.W) was formed in 1969 to review the labour welfare scheme, described it as social security measures which contribute to improving the conditions under which workers are employed in India.

Many acts such as the Factories Act of 1948, the Workmen's Compensation Act of 1923, the Maternity Benefit Act of 1961, Employees' State Insurance Act of 1948 which provides for sickness benefit, maternity benefit, disablement benefit, dependents' benefit, funeral benefit, medical benefit etc. have been passed which provide welfare facilities and social security to industrial workers.

The statutory basis for welfare facilities and social security is provided by the Factories Act of 1948. There is the provision under Section 49 (1) of the Factories Act of 1948 to appoint such number of welfare officers as may be prescribed in the Act. The welfare officers are entrusted with certain duties and they have to perform certain functions for the purpose of implementing welfare and social security programmes. The welfare officers play a very important role with respect to labour welfare and social security.

The role of a welfare officer can be described as an important link between the management or employer and workers. The labour officers have to safeguard the interest of their managements or employers and at the same time, they have to perform certain functions and duties for the well-being of the workers.

Labour officers are concerned with workers at work and with their cordial relationship within their organisations. The labour welfare officers make all the efforts to help workers develop their potentialities, capacities, to increase their efficiency and productivity by providing various welfare facilities as per the legislative provisions so that they can derive great satisfaction from their jobs. Moreover it is their responsibility to ensure compliances of all statutory schemes meant for the welfare of employees. So far as the role or importance of the welfare officers are concerned, the following aspects must be considered :

(a) The welfare aspect which is concerned with working conditions and amenities such as canteens, crèches housing recreation etc.

(b) The labour aspect which is concerned mainly with productivity, recruitment, placement etc.

(c) The industrial relations aspect which is concerned with the settlement of disputes, joint consultation etc.

From the functions and duties of the labour welfare officers and the discussion done so far, we now know the role of labour welfare officers. They are expected to play the role of counsellor, mentor (means trusted advisor), mediator, liaise between the management and labour for the well-being of workers. Hence, the importance of the role played by the welfare officers is largely due to the fact that the success of an organisation heavily depends on the services, work of the loyal employees or labour who have the genuine desire to be cooperative with the management and the welfare officers have much scope in this respect. The role of Welfare Officer can be understood by considering the following points :

a) The conscience role of the welfare officers is that of a humanitarian who always reminds the management of its moral and ethical obligations to workers.

b) The labour welfare officers play the role of a counsellor to whom the workers may approach for consultations and with whom they can discuss their marital, mental, health, physical problems.

c) As a mediator, a welfare officer plays the role of a peace maker, offering to settle the disputes that may arise among individuals or groups. He acts as a liaison and a communicating link between an individual and a group and also the workers and management.

d) To establish contacts and hold consultations for maintaining harmonious relations between factory management and workers. This role of welfare officers is important for the smooth working of the organisation.

e) The advisory role of a welfare officer is very important as it helps the management to formulate labour and welfare policies. Further, he can interpret the policies framed to the workers in the language they understand. This leads to remove the misunderstanding of workers if any and helps to maintain harmonious industrial relations.

(f)   As an advisor, the role of a welfare officer is quite important as far as the following points are concerned :

(i)   To provide advice for the fulfilment of necessary obligations in respect of statutory provisions of the Factories Act, 1948 and the Rules made thereunder relating to medical services concerning medical examination of employees, health records, supervision of hazardous jobs, processes etc, accident prevention, supervision of safety committees, investigations of accidents, workmen's compensation etc.

(ii)   To render advice and assist the management for the purpose of the fulfillment of statutory and non-statutory obligations relating to prevention of injuries, maintenance of safe and healthy work environment in those factories wherein safety officers are not required to be appointed under Section 40-B of the Factories Act of 1948.

(iii)   To advise the management and other departments of the factory in respect of working hours, compensation for sickness and injuries and various other welfare and social benefit measures.

(iv)   To give advice in order to encourage the provision of various amenities e.g. shelters for rest, rest-rooms, canteens, crèches, adequate latrine facilities, drinking water, gratuity payments etc.

(v)   To help the management in regulating the grant of leave and also to explain to the workers various legislative provision relating to leave and to guide them in matter of submitting the applications for regulating authorised absence.

(vi)   To suggest various measures which serve to increase the productivity, efficiency of workers and to raise the standard of living of workers and in promoting their well-being.

(viii)   To help and to give advice to the management on matters relating to training of new workers, apprentices, on transfers and promotions of workers already in service, workers' education etc.

Thus, the basic role of welfare officers is to promote the welfare of workers which is an important aspect of industrial relations. Their role is important because labour welfare facilities provide healthy working environment and help to develop a sense of belongingness towards organisation among workers. It makes workers more responsible and efficient.

It may be noted that as a welfare officer is appointed by the management and is paid by it, he is dependent on the management for many things; it is very difficult for him to be neutral.

2.5 DIFFERENCE BETWEEN PERSONNEL MANAGER AND WELFARE OFFICER

We have studied so far the functions, duties and qualifications of welfare officers, how they are appointed etc. Now we have to know the difference between 'Personnel Manager' and 'Welfare Officer'. But for the purpose, we must know meaning and nature of personnel management because the personnel manager works as the head of the personnel department and performs various functions and duties relating to personnel.

2.5.1 Meaning and Nature of 'Personnel Management'

Personnel management is a specialised branch of management, and so it necessarily follows the principles of management in general in addition to specific principles of Personnel Management. It can be best explained by considering some important definitions stated by the experts

(a) **Edwin B. Flippo :** "*Personnel Management is the planning, organising, directing and controlling of the procurement, development, compensation, integration, maintenance and separation of human resources to the end that individual, organisational and social objectives are accomplished*".

(b) **Wendell French :** "*Personnel Management is the recruitment, selection, development, utilisation of and accommodation to human resources by organisations. The human resources of an organisation consists of all individuals regardless of their role and who are engaged in any of the organisation's activities*".

(c) **C. H. Northcott :** "*Personnel Management is an extension of general management, that of prompting and stimulating every employee to make his fullest contribution to the purpose of business*".

(d) **Scott, Clothier and Spriegel :** "*Personnel Management is that branch of management which is responsible on a staff basis for concentrating on those aspects of operations which are primarily concerned with the relationship of management to employees and employees to employees and with the development of individual and the group. The objective is to attain maximum individual development, desirable working relationship between employers and employees, and effective moulding of human resources as contrasted with physical resources*'.

From these definitions, we get an idea about the subject-matter and nature of Personnel Management. It is the functional area of general management and management of people at work. It is concerned with recruitment, selection, development, proper utilisation of human resources by an organisation and it involves planning, co-ordination, communication, controlling, etc.

Effective utilisation of human resources is important and hence, personnel management considers that the development of individuals at work is very important and suggests to take necessary actions to develop the potentialities and capacities of the available human resources to the maximum possible extent. Personnel management is really a positive approach and philosophy of management and is basically concerned with the overall development of human resources for their optimum utilisation to achieve certain goals.

2.5.2 Terminology : The Name of the Game

Different terms such as 'Personnel Management', 'Labour Management', 'Manpower Management' etc. are found to be used interchangeably and 'Staff Executive', 'Personnel Manager', 'Personnel Administrator' etc. are the designations used for the person appointed for performing the duties and functions relating to personnel employed.

Richard Calhoon pointed out in his book, 'Managing Personnel' (1964) that, "From the earliest term 'employment manager' evolved the more general term of 'Personnel Manager' in the 1920s and 30s". Thereafter, the executives looking after personnel functions have been designated as 'Personnel Director', 'Personnel Executive', 'Staff and Personnel Manager', 'Labour Welfare Officer', 'Labour Liaison Officer', 'Personnel Manager' etc. However, in India, the Royal Commission on Labour in 1831 recommended to appoint 'Labour Officers'

The Royal Commission on Labour stated that, "We advocate for all factories the exclusion of the jobber from the engagement and dismissal of labour. This can best be achieved by the employment of a labour officer, and this is the course we recommend wherever the scale of factory permits it. He should be subordinate to no one except the General Manager of the factory, and should be carefully selected. Integrity, personality, energy, the gift of understanding individuals and linguistic facility are the main qualities required. No employee should be engaged except by the labour officer personally, in consultation with departmental heads, and none should be dismissed without his consent, except by the manager himself, after hearing what the labour officer has to say. It should be the business of the labour officer to ensure that no employee is discharged without adequate cause; if he is of the right type, the workers will rapidly learn to place confidence in him and to regard him as their friend. There are many other duties which such an officer can fulfil, particularly, in respect to welfare."

Thus, the post of labour officer was instituted initially to eliminate the evils and malpractices of the jobber system and to develop and improve labour administration in mills. In the 1930s, the cotton textile mills in Bombay and Jute industry in Calcutta pioneered the labour officers. These officers were instructed with maintaining law and order in an organisation. Later on, their functions gradually changed to welfare activities and they started introducing certain welfare services such as setting up of food-grain co-operatives, organisation of sports etc.

The Labour Investigation Committee of 1960 recommended for the institution of labour officers which had considerable impact on the policy of the government in respect of appointing welfare officers in the factories, mines etc. before independence. The government of India gave a serious thought to appoint welfare officers after 1947 and as a result, statutory provisions have been made to appoint welfare officers in factories, plantations and mines according to the provisions of the concerned acts i.e. the Factories Act of 1948, the Plantations Labour Act of 1951 and the Mines Act of 1952.

Thus, though in the past, the designations 'Personnel Manager' and 'Labour Welfare Officer' or 'Labour Officer' were used interchangeably after 1947 and passing of the Acts mentioned above the post of labour officer has become statutory.

Difference Between 'Personnel Manager' and 'Welfare Officer'

From the discussion done so far, one must have got an idea about personnel management. As the head of the personnel department, a personnel manager has to perform various functions besides the functions mentioned in the definitions. The functions, duties, role etc. of a welfare officer are already discussed. It is clear that there is difference between a personnel manager and a welfare officer so far as their status, mode of appointment, statutory status, functions and duties they perform etc. are concerned. Following are the points which make clear the difference between them :

(a) The appointment of a welfare officer is according to the provisions of Acts applicable and his post is statutory, while the personnel manager's post is not statutory. Moreover, additional and assistant welfare officers are required to be appointed considering the number of workers according to the Factory's Act of 1948. In respect of personnel managers, there is no such legislative provision.

(b) For a person to be appointed as a welfare officer, certain qualifications are prescribed in the Act and procedure is also laid down. The qualifications, experience of a person to be appointed as a personnel manager is decided by an organisation which appoints a person as the 'Personnel Manager' and the organisation decides the procedure of selection of a personnel manager.

(c) A personnel manager has to perform many functions such as managerial functions which include planning, organising, directing, controlling etc., operative functions which include procurement of personnel function, the development function, the compensating function, the integration function, maintenance function, separation function etc. But the functions of a welfare officer are limited to labour welfare, labour administration and maintenance of labour relations.

(d) A personnel manager is the head of the Personnel Department while a welfare officer is subordinate to the personnel manager. In this respect, the role of a welfare officer is of advisory nature.

(e) The basic role of a personnel manager is the management of manpower resources and is mainly concerned with leadership both in group and individual relationships and labour management relations. He has to make arrangement for selection and recruitment of employees according to manpower planning. A welfare officer can only assist him in this respect by making available necessary information in this regard.

Any matter which needs someone's attention and which nobody wants to deal with it often handled by the personnel department. Such activities may be peripheral i.e. outside of a sphere but important and crucial for the efficient and effective operation of an organisation. This aspect is out of the scope of functions of a welfare officer.

(f) A labour officer mainly concerns himself with the implementation of labour laws and the maintenance of proper working conditions, with matters connected with well-being of workers and with promotion of harmonious and peaceful labour-management relations. Besides this, a personnel manager concerns himself with many other matters and functions for which a welfare officer can not be held responsible. His is mainly a staff function with the role of staff-advisor or specialist. He is expected to act as an advisor, counsellor, mediator and liaison-man between the personnel manager and labour.

(g) A personnel manager has to perform various duties considering the functions he has to perform. His duties cover wide areas not stated in any Act. His duties are mainly related to manpower planning, recruitment and selection of employees, job evaluation, motivation, organisational planning and development etc. But so far as the duties of a welfare officer are concerned, the state government is empowered to prescribe the duties and conditions of service of a welfare officer. Hence, at present the duties of a welfare officer are mainly confined to welfare work. The Central Model Rules 1957 laid down certain duties for labour welfare officers. Further, in exercise of the powers conferred by Section 49 (2), Sections 50 and 112 of the Factories Act of 1948, the government of Maharashtra has made certain rules making clear the duties of the welfare officers which we have already considered.

(h) A personnel manager is more concerned with helping the employees to develop their potentialities and capacities to the maximum possible extent so that they can derive great satisfaction from their jobs by taking into consideration capacities, interests, opportunities etc. of the employees. While the welfare officers look after welfare activities which also help the employees to get satisfaction. But the scope of making efforts is wider for the personnel manager than the labour welfare officer.

(i) Since recruitment, selection, development and utilisation of the employees' skills and efficiency are an integral part of any organised effort and a personnel manager is directly concerned with that while a labour welfare officer is not.

(j) To be successful in his job, a personnel manager should be a specialist in organisation theory and as such, he must be an effective advisor to top management in organisational matters and must be able to organise his own department properly. A welfare officer, on the other hand, assists the personnel management in framing policies related to the welfare of the workers.

It can be concluded that the nature of duties, functions, role of a personnel manager and that of a welfare officer is different. The functions, duties and role of a personnel manager is more comprehensive and not limited to the welfare of workers. Welfare officers have to perform duties according to the provisions of the related acts. Welfare officers concentrate on welfare measures, programmes and also help to solve problems and grievances of workers in order to maintain good industrial relations and peace.

According to the National Commission on Labour, the care of workers in all matters affecting their well-being, both at place of work and outside puts a special responsibility on the welfare officer. He should be a maintenance engineer of humans. Of course, it is also found than in many cases, he also handles grievances and complaints of workers relating to terms and conditions of service and other matters which lie in the domain of personnel management. Therefore, it can be said that virtually, there is no strict demarcation between personnel functions and welfare functions. The difference is likely to stay between them because of the statutory status and position of a welfare officer.

POINTS TO REMEMBER

1. **Qualifications of Labour Welfare Officer**

   (a) A University degree or a Master's degree.

   (b) Degree or diploma in social sciences, social works or social welfare from any recognised Institution/University.

   (c) An adequate knowledge of the language spoken by the majority of the workers in the area where the factories, mills and plantations are situated.

2. **Appointment and Qualifications of 'Welfare Officer' According to the Maharashtra Welfare Officers (Duties, Qualifications and Conditions of Service) Rules of 1966**

   (a) Has obtained a degree or diploma in social science recognised by the State Government in this behalf, has qualified at a viva voce test conducted by the Chief Inspector of the Factories, Mumbai as provided. This test consists of a test of general knowledge and in particular of labour problems pertaining to the Maharashtra state.

   (b) Has adequate knowledge of Marathi language.

   (c) No person who is directly or indirectly interested in any factory or in any patent or machinery connected with it shall be appointed as the Welfare Officer, the Additional Welfare Officer or Assistant Welfare Officer and he shall be allowed to hold such office after he becomes so interested in the factory.

3. Functions of Labour Welfare Officer

It mainly includes labour welfare advice and assistance in implementing legislative as well as non-legislative provisions relating to following matters or aspects :

(a) Health and safety measures.

(b) Sanitation and cleanliness.

(c) Welfare amenities.

(d) Working conditions.

(e) Recreation of workers.

(f) Various services like housing, provision of grains, other commodities etc.

(g) Formation of welfare committees.

(h) Lighting facilities.

(i) Implementation of Welfare Acts.

4. Duties of Labour Welfare Officer

(a) To help and maintain harmonious relations between management and workers.

(b) Redressal of workers' grievances.

(c) To watch industrial relations and to settle disputes by persuasive efforts.

(d) To provide feedback to management regarding labour's point of view to shape and formulate necessary labour policies and also to interpret these policies to the workers.

(e) To advice management on the implementation of health and safety programmes for the welfare of labour.

(f) To introduce and implement various measures for promoting productive efficiency of labour.

(g) To ameliorate the working conditions of workers.

(h) To help the workers to adjust and adapt themselves to working environment.

(i) Personnel counselling and advising workers on their individual personal problems.

5. Role of Labour Welfare Officer

(a) The welfare aspect which is concerned with working conditions and amenities such as canteens, crèches housing recreation etc.

(b) The labour aspect which is concerned mainly with productivity, recruitment, placement etc.

(c) The industrial relations aspect which is concerned with the settlement of disputes, joint consultation etc.

(e) The conscience role of the welfare officers is that of a humanitarian who always reminds the management of its moral and ethical obligations to workers.

(f) The labour welfare officers play the role of a counsellor to whom the workers may approach for consultations and with whom they can discuss their marital, mental, health, physical problems.

(g) As a mediator, a welfare officer plays the role of a peace maker, offering to settle the disputes that may arise among individuals or groups. He acts as a liaison and a communicating link between an individual and a group and also workers and management.

(h) To establish contacts and hold consultations for maintaining harmonious relations between factory management and workers. This role of welfare officers is important for the smooth working of the organisation.

(i) The advisory role of a welfare officer is very important as it helps the management to formulate labour and welfare policies. Further, he can interpret the policies framed to the workers in the language they understand. This leads to remove the misunderstanding of workers if any and helps to maintain harmonious industrial relations.

QUESTIONS FOR DISCUSSION

Q.1 How is a Welfare Officer appointed? What are the qualifications required for the appointment of a Labour Welfare Officer?

Q.2 Explain the functions and duties of a Labour Welfare Officer.

Q.3 Explain the functions and role of a Labour Welfare Officer.

Q.4 Explain the difference between a Personnel Manager and a Labour Welfare Officer.

Q.5 Write notes on the following :

(a) Appointment and qualifications of a Labour Welfare Officer.

(b) Functions and duties of a Labour Welfare Officer.

(c) Role of a Labour Welfare Officer.

QUESTIONS FROM PREVIOUS EXAMINATIONS

Q.1 Explain the role, functions and duties of the Welfare Officer.   **[Dec-2012]**

Q.2 Examine the functions and duties of the Labour Welfare Officer.   **[April-2013]**

Q.3 Distinguish between : Labour Welfare Officer and Personnel Manager.

Q.4 Elaborate the Qualifications and Duties of Labour Welfare.   **[April-2006]**

Q.5 What are the Duties of a Welfare Officer?   **[Dec-2007]**

Q.6 Examine the Functions and Duties of a Labour Welfare Officer.   **[April-2009]**

Q.7 Explain the Role, Qualifications, Functions and Duties of the Welfare Officer.

[Dec-2010]

Chapter 3...

Welfare Amenities

Contents ...

Learning Objectives

At the end of the chapter, you will understand :

- Various welfare amenities provided to labour.

- The classification of welfare amenities.

- The statutory and non-statutory labour welfare amenities.

- Role and approach of the government in respect of labour welfare and health.

- Various agencies for labour welfare.

- Statutory and non-statutory labour welfare amenities.

- Role and approach of the government in respect of labour welfare and health.

- Various agencies for providing labour welfare amenities.

- Role of employers, trade unions and voluntary organisations in providing labour welfare amenities.

health, emergency medical care etc. Provision of first-aid appliances, medical appliances has been made in the Factories Act, the Mine Act and the Motor Transport Workers Act. It is the statutory obligation on the employers to provide first-aid boxes equipped with the prescribed contents as per the provisions of the Acts.

The Employees' State Insurance Act of 1948 extends various benefits to industrial workers. Important benefits provided under the Act are disablement benefits, maternity benefits, dependents benefits, sickness benefits, medical benefits etc. The families of workers coming under the purview of the Act are also covered to some extent.

Some of the employers in big undertakings voluntarily provide comprehensive and health facilities. Apart from the medical and health facilities provided by legislation and by some employers on a voluntary basis, some labour welfare centres and some trade unions also provide certain health and medical services.

(f) Health Services in Respect of Dangerous Operations : Section 87 of the Factories Act of 1948 refers to dangerous operations. If the Government is of the opinion that any manufacturing process or operation carried on in a factory exposes the persons employed in it to a serious risk of bodily injury, poisoning or disease, it may make rules applicable to any factory or class or description of factories in which a manufacturing process or operation is carried on :

(i)   Specifying the manufacturing process or operation and declaring it to be dangerous.

(ii)   Prohibiting or restricting the employment of women, adolescents or children in the manufacturing process or operation.

(iii) Providing for the periodical medical examination of persons employed, or seeking to be employed, in the manufacturing process or operation and prohibiting the employment of persons not certified as fit for such employment and requiring the payment by the occupier of the factory of fees for such medical examination.

(iv)   Providing for the protection of all persons employed in the manufacturing process or operation or in the vicinity of the places where it is carried on.

(v)   Prohibiting, restricting or controlling the use of any specified materials or process in connection with the manufacturing process or operation.

(vi)   Requiring the provision of additional welfare amenities and sanitary facilities and the supply of protective equipment and clothing, and laying down the standards thereof, having regard to the dangerous nature of the manufacturing process or operation.

Thus, these provisions make clear that the main function of health services is to protect workers against the health hazards arising out of the nature of their work or the work environment and these services include carrying out periodical medical examination to detect early signs of ill-health and to prevent the out break of serious health complaints.

(g) Facilities in Respect of Latrines, Urinals and Spittoons : One of the outstanding features of the Factories Act, 1948 is the provision for health, safety and welfare of the workers.

The Act makes various provisions in regard to matters relating to health as well as safety and welfare of the workers. These provisions imposed certain obligations upon occupiers or managers of factories to protect workers from accidents and to secure for them conditions conducive to their health, safety and welfare in the premises where they work.

It is obligatory for the managers or the occupiers to maintain necessary inspecting staff and to make necessary provision for maintaining health, cleanliness etc. and also provide certain amenities such as ventilation, light, drinking water, latrines and urinals etc.

I.   **Latrines and Urinals [Section 19]**

(1) **In Every Factory :**

(a) Sufficient Latrine and also urinal accommodation of prescribed types must be provided conveniently situated and accessible to workers at all times while they are at the factory.

(b) Separate enclosed accommodation is required to be provided for male as well as for female workers.

(c) Such accommodation must be adequately lighted and properly ventilated. No latrine or urinal shall, unless specially exempted in writing by the Chief Inspector, be in communication with any workroom except through an intervening open space or passage which is adequately ventilated.

(d) All such accommodation must be maintained in a clean and sanitary condition at all times.

(e) Sweepers must be employed whose primary duty would be to keep latrines, urinals and washing places clean.

(2) **In Every Factory Wherein more than Two Hundred and Fifty Workers are Ordinarily Employed :**

(a) All latrine and urinal accommodations shall be of prescribed sanitary types only.

(b) The floors and internals walls, up to the height of ninety centimetres, of the latrines and urinals and also of the sanitary blocks shall be laid in glazed tiles or otherwise finished to provide a smooth polished impervious surface.

(3) The State Government may prescribe the number of latrines and urinals to be provided in any factory in proportion to the number of female and male workers ordinarily employed therein and provide for such further matters in respect of sanitation in factories, including the obligation of workers in this regard as the State Government considers it necessary in the interest of the health of workers employed therein.

3.1 INTRODUCTION

Labour welfare is one of the major aspects of national programmes towards bettering the lot of labour and creating a life and work environment of decent comfort for this class of population.

Various measures and activities undertaken by the government, employers, association of workers and welfare amenities provided by them for the improvement of workers' standards of life, increasing their efficiency and productivity, and for the promotion of their economic and social well-being are labelled as **'Welfare Work'**.

The International Labour Organisation stated in its report that, **"Workers' welfare** should be understood as meaning *such services, facilities and amenities which may be established in or in vicinity of undertaking to enable the persons employed in them to perform their work in healthy, congenial (i.e. pleasant) surroundings and provided with amenities conducive to good health and high morale."* This makes clear the importance of labour welfare amenities and therefore welfare amenities must be provided to workers. However, for maximum results, welfare activities providing welfare amenities have to be undertaken in the right spirit i.e. mainly with a view to making the lives of the workers happier and healthier.

Various welfare amenities are provided under different legislations in India Welfare. They are known as statutory welfare measures. Besides those welfare amenities, the employers, non-government organisations (NGOs) also provide certain welfare amenities known as non-statutory labour welfare amenities. Let us consider important labour welfare amenities in this chapter.

3.2 VARIOUS WELFARE AMENITIES PROVIDED TO LABOUR

In the main report of the Labour Investigation Committee, 1946, many labour welfare amenities have been mentioned. They have become a part of statutory obligations of the employers. The statutory welfare amenities and facilities are provided in India under different Acts, e.g. the Factories Act of 1948, the Plantation Labour Act of 1951, the Mines Act of 1951 etc. There are also provisions in the Acts to appoint a suitably qualified person as a welfare officer according to the provisions of the Acts who performs certain functions and duties as prescribed. Besides that the employers and workers' organisations also provide the welfare amenities and facilities. The important amenities and facilities are given below :

(a) Hygienic Facilities and Amenities in Respect of Sanitation : It is necessary to maintain clean, sanitary and hygienic working conditions and environment. As such it is very important to provide the basic welfare amenities relating to toilets, water for drinking and washing, facilities for storing and drying wet clothing. These amenities are essential in India because of its hot and humid climate.

Most of our Indian workers generally come from a rural background and are not very educated. Therefore, they also require to get education for using various hygienic facilities effectively.

In respect of these facilities, provisions have been made in the Acts, e.g. the Factories Act of 1948, the Contract Labour (Regulation and Abolition) Act of 1970 and Rules made thereunder.

(b) Shelters and Rest Rooms : These amenities help to reduce fatigue of workers and contribute to their comfort and efficiency.

Every factory has to provide necessary sitting arrangements for workers who have to work in a standing position. It enables them to take rest for a while in the course of their work.

Rest rooms are essential so that the workers may relax during their breaks for rest and meals. They can also wait till the time they start their work, especially before or after late shifts.

(c) Lunch Rooms : Lunch rooms or mess rooms are elementary feeding facilities where workers can sit and eat the food in comfort which they bring from their homes. Now, it is found that great importance is attached to the provisions of canteens in which food and tea, coffee etc. are provided to workers at subsidised rates.

(d) Crèche and Wash Rooms for the Children : This is a welfare facility which is provided for women workers. *A crèche is defined as a place where babies of working mothers are taken care of while their mothers are at work.*

The need for setting up crèches in industrial establishments was stressed by the Royal Commission on Labour in 1931. Thereafter, the provision of a crèche was first made in the Factories Act of 1934 and its need was emphasised in the Factories Act of 1948. The provision of crèche is made in the Act in Section 48. In the Plantation Labour Act of 1961, there is provision of crèches in Section 12. The Acts empower the State Governments to prescribe rules for the location of and the standards to be maintained in respect of crèches including facilities for working, changing clothes, free milk, refreshments etc. A crèche must be a well maintained and adequately lighted, ventilated room which should be in clean and sanitary condition. It is also provided in the Act that children below six years of age should be under the charge of a woman trained in care of children and infants.

(e) Health Services and First-aid Appliances : The International Labour Organisation emphasised the importance of industrial health care. The Royal Commission on Labour in 1931 and the Labour Investigation Committee in 1946 underlined the necessity of providing basic health and welfare amenities.

The importance of industrial health services is greater in India than elsewhere. It is so because of the adverse effects of an unhealthy work environment in many factories, plantations etc., because of the incidence of tropical diseases, long hours of work, malnutrition because of low wages, ignorance and poverty among the workers. Therefore, there was felt the dire need to provide health services which include health and medical facilities. The health amenities cover first-aid, ambulance, industrial hygiene, occupational health, emergency medical care etc. Provision of first-aid appliances, medical appliances has been made in the Factories Act, the Mine Act and the Motor Transport Workers Act. It is the statutory obligation on the employers to provide first-aid boxes equipped with the prescribed contents as per the provisions of the Acts.

The Employees' State Insurance Act of 1948 extends various benefits to industrial workers. Important benefits provided under the Act are disablement benefits, maternity benefits, dependents benefits, sickness benefits, medical benefits etc. The families of workers coming under the purview of the Act are also covered to some extent.

Some of the employers in big undertakings voluntarily provide comprehensive and health facilities. Apart from the medical and health facilities provided by legislation and by some employers on a voluntary basis, some labour welfare centres and some trade unions also provide certain health and medical services.

(f) Health Services in Respect of Dangerous Operations : Section 87 of the Factories Act of 1948 refers to dangerous operations. If the Government is of the opinion that any manufacturing process or operation carried on in a factory exposes the persons employed in it to a serious risk of bodily injury, poisoning or disease, it may make rules applicable to any factory or class or description of factories in which a manufacturing process or operation is carried on :

(i) Specifying the manufacturing process or operation and declaring it to be dangerous.

(ii) Prohibiting or restricting the employment of women, adolescents or children in the manufacturing process or operation.

(iii) Providing for the periodical medical examination of persons employed, or seeking to be employed, in the manufacturing process or operation and prohibiting the employment of persons not certified as fit for such employment and requiring the payment by the occupier of the factory of fees for such medical examination

(iv) Providing for the protection of all persons employed in the manufacturing process or operation or in the vicinity of the places where it is carried on.

(v) Prohibiting, restricting or controlling the use of any specified materials or process in connection with the manufacturing process or operation.

(vi) Requiring the provision of additional welfare amenities and sanitary facilities and the supply of protective equipment and clothing, and laying down the standards thereof, having regard to the dangerous nature of the manufacturing process or operation.

Thus, these provisions make clear that the main function of health services is to protect workers against the health hazards arising out of the nature of their work or the work environment and these services include carrying out periodical medical examination to detect early signs of ill-health and to prevent the out break of serious health complaints.

(g) Facilities in Respect of Latrines, Urinals and Spittoons : One of the outstanding features of the Factories Act, 1948 is the provision for health, safety and welfare of the workers.

The Act makes various provisions in regard to matters relating to health as well as safety and welfare of the workers. These provisions imposed certain obligations upon occupiers or managers of factories to protect workers from accidents and to secure for them conditions conducive to their health, safety and welfare in the premises where they work.

It is obligatory for the managers or the occupiers to maintain necessary inspecting staff and to make necessary provision for maintaining health, cleanliness etc. and also provide certain amenities such as ventilation, light, drinking water, latrines and urinals etc.

I.   **Latrines and Urinals [Section 19]**

    (1)   In Every Factory :

    (a)   Sufficient Latrine and also urinal accommodation of prescribed types must be provided conveniently situated and accessible to workers at all times while they are at the factory.

    (b)   Separate enclosed accommodation is required to be provided for male as well as for female workers.

    (c)   Such accommodation must be adequately lighted and properly ventilated. No latrine or urinal shall, unless specially exempted in writing by the Chief Inspector, be in communication with any workroom except through an intervening open space or passage which is adequately ventilated.

    (d)   All such accommodation must be maintained in a clean and sanitary condition at all times.

    (e)   Sweepers must be employed whose primary duty would be to keep latrines, urinals and washing places clean.

    (2)   In Every Factory Wherein more than Two Hundred and Fifty Workers are Ordinarily Employed :

    (a)   All latrine and urinal accommodations shall be of prescribed sanitary types only.

    (b)   The floors and internals walls, up to the height of ninety centimetres, of the latrines and urinals and also of the sanitary blocks shall be laid in glazed tiles or otherwise finished to provide a smooth polished impervious surface.

    (3)   The State Government may prescribe the number of latrines and urinals to be provided in any factory in proportion to the number of female and male workers ordinarily employed therein and provide for such further matters in respect of sanitation in factories, including the obligation of workers in this regard as the State Government considers it necessary in the interest of the health of workers employed therein.

II. Spittoons [Section 20]

(1) In every factory, there must be provided a sufficient number of spittoons in convenient places and they must be maintained in a clean and hygienic condition.

(2) The State Government may make a rule prescribing the type and the number of spittoons to be provided and their location in any factory and provide for such further matters relating to their maintenance in a clean and hygienic condition.

(3) No person shall spit within the premises of a factory except in the spittoons provided for that purpose and a notice containing this provision and the penalty for its violation must be prominently displayed at suitable places in the premises of the factory.

(4) Whoever spits in contravention of Sub-section (3) of Section 20 shall be punishable with a fine not exceeding Rupees five.

It is obvious that the intention of the Sub-section (4) of Section 20 is to enforce and promote the discipline amongst the employees of any factory and therefore the provision is made that any one splitting in contravention of Sub-section (3) of Section 20 will do so at the pain of punishment. Welfare facilities, amenities are also voluntarily provided by the employers. Now let us consider some of the important welfare facilities voluntarily provided by employers.

(h) Transport Facilities : Transport facilities for workers residing at long distances are essential to relieve them from strain and anxiety. These facilities definitely add to the welfare of labour. They also help to reduce the rate of absenteeism.

It is found that in almost all countries in the world, mobility of workers has become possible by modern transportation means. In this respect, road and rail transport have acquired considerable significance.

Many undertakings in private sectors e.g. Godrej, Sardoz, L & T, Voltas, Philips provide transport facilities to their employees. Some public sector enterprises also provide transport facilities to their employees. Some organisations also grant local conveyance allowance to their employees.

(i) Educational Facilities : Many organisations provide educational facilities to their workers and their children of workers in the form of schools, reading rooms, libraries, financial assistance etc.

Improvement in the quality of the work force demands accelerated pace of economic and industrial development for which educational facilities to workers, their families and their children are very essential.

(j) Medical Facilities : Medical facilities are provided to workers and their families by many private sector undertakings, organisations voluntarily in the form of suitably equipped first-aid centres, ambulance rooms, dispensaries, for the treatment of diseases like T.B., cancer, leprosy, mental diseases etc. Some of such private companies are TELCO, TISCO, Hindustan Lever, Godrej, L & T, the Mafatlal Group which have extended medical amenities to their employees.

(k) Housing Facilities : Housing facilities are made available to employees in the form of self-contained tenements with basic facilities like sanitation, running water supply, electricity etc. Such facilities are provided by some industrial employers both in public and private sectors. Some of the member mills of the Mumbai Mill Owners' Association provided tenements to their workers.

There are housing colonies of companies such as TELCO, L & T, Godrej, HMT. The Tata Iron and Steel Company [TISCO] had build more than 20,000 residential quarters which were provided to about 45,000 employees in Jamshedpur.

(l) Recreational Facilities : Recreational facilities are important from the viewpoint of welfare of workers. Recreation is, in fact, a leisure time activity. It refreshes an individual mentally and lessens the monotony and drudgery of his day to day work. 'Drudge' means a person who does laborious or mental work. Music, drama, dance, games and sports, paintings etc. are different forms of recreation. These facilities create a healthy climate for industrial peace and progress.

In India, various recreational facilities have been provided in more than one way statutorily, voluntarily by employers and also by social welfare agencies and trade unions.

Recreational amenities are provided by the organisations either inside or near the work places.

(m) Co-operative Societies : These societies help their members according to the objectives for which they are established. The institution of co-operative stores, fair price shops play an important role in providing workers' with essential items of need. These societies provide to their members good quality of food grains and other essential goods and services at fair and reasonable prices.

3.3 CLASSIFICATION OF LABOUR WELFARE AMENITIES

The meaning of labour welfare can be made more clear by listing various labour amenities and facilities which are generally referred to as welfare measures or welfare work. A comprehensive list of welfare facilities is given by the Committee of Experts on Welfare Facilities for Industrial Workers convened by the ILO in 1963.

Prof. M. V. Moorthy also stated welfare measures in his book, **"Principles of Labour Welfare"** by dividing these measures in two broad groups on the line of classification made by the Committee referred to above. The classification, thus, adopted, is given below :

(1)   Welfare amenities or measures inside the work place or within the precincts of the establishments, and

(2)   Welfare amenities or measures outside the work place or establishment.

Each of the above mentioned groups include several labour welfare amenities.

Labour welfare amenities which are provided inside the work place are mentioned below :

(i)   Latrines and urinals.

(ii)   Washing and bathing facilities.

(iii) Crèches.

(iv)   Rest shelters.

(v)   Arrangements for drinking water.

(vi)   Arrangements for prevention of fatigue.

(vii) Health service including occupational safety.

(viii) Administrative arrangements within a plant to look after welfare.

(ix)   Uniforms and protective clothing.

(x)   Shift allowance.

(xi)   Recreational facilities made available inside the establishment.

(xii) Canteen services.

(xiii) Co-operatives, loans, financial grants, saving schemes etc.

(xiv) Women and child welfare amenities.

(xv)   Management of workers' cloak-rooms, reading room and library.

Labour welfare amenities which are provided outside the work place or the establishment are as follows :

(i)   Maternity benefits.

(ii)   Social insurance measures, including gratuity, pension, provident fund and rehabilitation.

(iii) Benevolent funds.

(iv)   Medical facilities, including programmes for physical fitness and efficiency, family planning and child welfare.

(v)   Education facilities such as schools, nursery, etc. including adult education.

(vi)   Housing facilities.

(vii) Recreational facilities, including sports, cultural activities, library and reading room; provided outside the establishment.

(viii) Holiday homes and leave travel facilities.

(ix)   Workers' co-operatives, including consumers' co-operative stores, fair price shops and co-operative thrift and credit societies.

(x)   Vocational training for dependants of workers.

(xi)   Other programmes for the welfare of women, youth and children.

(xii)   Transport to and from the place of work.

(xiii)   Roads, grounds, parks.

(xiv)   Watch and ward securities.

(xv)   Community, cultural, leadership development.

The above mentioned labour welfare facilities, amenities, activities may also be categorised as :

(a)   Intra-mural facilities or activities, and

(b)   Extra-mural facilities or activities.

(a) Intra-mural Facilities : It consists of various amenities provided within the factories or establishments and they include medical amenities, compensation for accidents, provision of crèches, supply of drinking water, washing and bathing facilities, provision of safety measures, various activities for the purpose of improving the conditions of employment etc.

(b) Extra-mural Facilities : It covers the services and facilities provided outside the establishments or factories such as housing accommodations, outdoor and indoor recreational facilities, amusement and sports, educational facilities, transport facilities, holiday homes etc.

The study team appointed by the Government of India in 1959 to examine the labour welfare activities then existing divided the entire range of these activities into three groups, viz.,

(i)   **Welfare Within the Precincts of an Establishment :** Medical aid, crèches, canteens, supply of drinking water.

(ii)   **Welfare Outside the Establishment :** Provision for indoor and outdoor recreation, housing, adult education, visual instruction, visual instructions.

(iii)   **Social Security.**

3.3.1 Classification of Labour Welfare Amenities on the Basis of Statutory and Non-Statutory Provisions

Employers in India are required statutorily to comply with the provisions of various welfare amenities under different legislation. They are mandatory and hence are called as statutory welfare provisions.

The statutory welfare amenities or measures are classified further into two categories which are as follows :

(1)   There are certain labour welfare amenities which are required to be provided irrespective of the size of the establishment or number of persons employed therein. These amenities include washing, storing and drying the clothing, first-aid boxes and appliances, drinking water, latrines and urinals etc.

(2) Certain labour welfare amenities are required to be provided subject to the specified number of persons. These facilities include canteen, rest shelter, crèches, ambulance room etc.

In the case of certain amenities, there are no minimum standards laid down as in the sphere of housing, medical treatment, recreation, transport, educational facilities etc. That is left to the discretion of the employers.

Non-statutory provisions are not mandatory. Therefore, they are called voluntary benefits or voluntary welfare measures. These voluntary labour welfare amenities are provided to the employees by their employers and also by the workers' organisations. Such amenities include house building, leave travel concession, fair price shops, loans for purchasing conveyance and so on.

3.4 STATUTORY AND NON-STATUTORY LABOUR WELFARE AMENITIES

We have considered above the classification of labour welfare amenities or facilities based on the basis of statutory and non-statutory provisions. Now let us consider these amenities in detail.

3.4.1 Statutory Labour Welfare Amenities

The statutory labour welfare provisions are mandated by the Factories Act, 1948, the Mines Act, 1952, the Plantation Labour Act, 1951, The Motor Transport Workers' Act, 1961, the Contract Labour (Regulation and Abolition) Act, 1970, the Merchant Shipping Act, 1958, the Dock Workers (Safety, health and welfare) scheme, 1961 and Inter-State Migrant Workmen (Regulation of Employment and Conditions of Service) Act 1979. Of all these Acts, the Factories Act is more significant.

The Factories Act was first conceived in 1881 when legislation was enacted to protect children and to provide health and safety measures. Later on, hours of work were sought to be regulated and were incorporated in the Act of 1911. The Act was amended following the recommendations of the Royal Commission of Labour and a more comprehensive legislation to regulate working conditions replaced the Factories Act in 1948. The Provision has been made in the Act to appoint a Labour Welfare Officer stating his duties.

We have already considered the various welfare amenities provided to laboured. A brief outline of various welfare facilities provided under different labour Acts mentioned above is given below :

(1) The Factories Act of 1948 : The welfare amenities which are provided under the Act are as follows. Certain welfare amenities are to be provided subject to the specified number of workers :

(a) Washing facilities (Section 42).

(b) Facilities for storing and dry clothing (Section 43).

(c) Sitting facilities for occasional rest for workers who are obliged to work standing (Section 44).

(d) First-aid boxes or cupboards – one for every 150 workers and ambulance facilities if there are more than 500 workers (Section 45).

(e) Canteens if employing more than 250 workers (Section 46).

(f) Shelters, rest rooms and lunch rooms, if employing over 150 workers (Section 47).

(g) Crèche, if employing more than 30 women (Section 48).

(h) Welfare Officer, if employing 500 or more workers (Section 49).

(2) The Mines Act, 1952 and the Mines Rules : The important obligations of the mine owners regarding health and welfare of their workers are given below :

(a) Maintenance of crèches where 50 women workers are employed.

(b) Provision of shelters for taking food and rest if 150 or more persons are employed.

(c) Provision of a canteen in mines employing 250 or more workers.

(d) Maintenance of first-aid boxes and first-aid rooms in mines employing more than 150 workers.

(e) Provision in coal mines of :

    (i) Pit head baths equipped with shower baths.

    (ii) Sanitary latrines.

    (iii) Lockers, separately for men and women workers.

(f) Appointment of a Welfare Officer in mines employing more than 500 or more persons to look after the matters relating to the welfare of the workers.

(3) The Plantations Labour Act, 1951 : The following welfare measures are required to be provided to the plantation workers under this Act :

(a) Canteens in plantations employing 150 or more workers (Section 11).

(b) Crèches in plantations employing 50 or more women workers (Section 12).

(c) Recreational facilities for the workers and their children (Section 13).

(d) Educational facilities in the estate for the children of workers, where there are 25 workers' children between the age of 6 and 12 (Section 14).

(e) Housing facilities for every worker and his family residing in the plantation. The standard and specification of the accommodation, procedure for allotment and rent chargeable from workers, are to be prescribed in the Rules by the State Governments (Section 15 and Section 16).

(f) The State Government may make rules requiring every plantation employer to provide the workers with such number and type of umbrellas, blankets, raincoats or other like amenities for the protection of workers from rain or cold as may be prescribed (Section 17).

(g) Appointment of a Welfare Officer in plantations employing 300 or more workers (Section 18).

The exact standards of these facilities have been prescribed under the Rules framed by the state governments.

(4) The Motor Transport Workers Act, 1961 : The Motor Transport Undertakings are required to provide certain welfare and health measures as per the provisions of the Act. These measures are as follows :

(a) Canteens of prescribed standard, if employing 100 or more workers (Section 8).

(b) Clean, ventilated, well-lighted and comfortable rest rooms at every place wherein motor transport workers are required to halt at night (Section 9).

(c) Uniforms, raincoats to drivers, conductors and line checking staff for protection against rain and cold. A prescribed amount of washing allowance is to be given to the above mentioned categories of staff (Section 10).

(d) Medical facilities are to be provided to the motor transport workers at the operating centres and at halting stations as may be prescribed by the State Government (Section 11).

(e) First-aid facilities equipped with the prescribed contents are to be provided in every transport vehicle (Section 12).

(5) The Contract Labour (Regulation and Abolition) Act, 1970 : The following welfare and health measures are to be provided to the contract workers by the contractor under this Act :

(a) A canteen in every establishment employing 100 or more workers. (Section 16).

(b) Rest rooms or other suitable alternative accommodation where the contract labour is required to halt at night in connection with the work of an establishment. (Section 17).

(c) Provision for a sufficient supply of wholesome drinking water, sufficient number of latrines and urinals of prescribed types and washing facilities. (Section 18)

(d) Provision for first-aid box equipped with the prescribed contents. (Section 19)

It is very important to note that the Act imposes liability on the principal employer to provide the above amenities to the contract labour employed in his establishment, if the contractor fails to do so.

(6) The Merchant Shipping Act, 1958 : Provisions in the Act relating to health and welfare cover the following labour amenities and measures are :

(a) Crew accommodation.

(b) Supply of sufficient drinking water.

(c) Supply of necessities like beddings, towels, mess utensils.

(d) Supply of medicines, medical stores, and provision of surgical and medical advice.

(e) Maintenance of proper weights and measures on board; and grant of relief to distressed seamen aboard a ship.

(f) Every foreign-going ship carrying more than the prescribed number of persons, including the crew, is required to have on board as part of her complement a qualified medical officer.

(g) Appointment of a Seamen's Welfare Officer at such ports in or outside India as the government may consider necessary.

(h) Establishment of hostels, clubs, canteens, and libraries.

(i) Provision of medical treatment and hospitals.

(j) Provision of educational facilities.

The governments have been authorized to frame rules, *inter alia*, for the levy of fees payable by owners of ships at prescribed rates for the purpose of providing amenities to seamen and for taking other measures for their welfare.

(7) Dock Workers (Safety, Health and Welfare) Scheme, 1961 : A comprehensive Dock Workers (Safety, Health and Welfare) Scheme, 1961, has been framed for all major ports and is administered by the Chief Advisor, Factories (Factory Advice Service and Labour Institutes).

It is framed under the Dock Workers (Regulation of Employment) Act, 1948. Amenities provided in the port premises include provision of :

(a) Urinals and latrines.

(b) Drinking water.

(c) Washing facilities.

(d) Bathing facilities.

(e) Canteens.

(f) Rest shelters.

(g) Call stands.

(h) First-aid arrangements.

Other welfare measures provided are :

(a) Housing

(b) Schools

(c) Educational facilities

(d) Grant of scholarships

(e) Libraries

(f)   Sports and recreation

(g)   Fair price shops,

(h)   Co-operative societies.

Cost of amenities, welfare and health measures and recreation facilities for registered workers shall be met from a separate fund called the **Dock Workers' Welfare Fund** which shall be maintained by the Board. Contributions to this Fund shall be made by all registered employers at such rate as may be determined by the Board. The Board shall frame rules for contributions for the maintenance and operation of the Fund. Different rates of welfare levy at different ports have been fixed.

The Dock Workers (Safety, Health and Welfare) Act, 1986 was enacted on 14th April, 1987. The Dock Workers (Safety, Health and Welfare) Rules, 1990 and Regulations, 1990 were framed under the new Act. As a result of introduction of these new set of statutes, the scope of dock work has considerably increased covering more number of workers employed in ports, who are hitherto not covered for their safety, health and welfare.

In addition, the Manufacture, Storage, and Import of Hazardous Chemicals Rules, 1989 framed under the Environment (Protection) Act, 1986 are also enforced by DGFASLI (Directorate General, Factory Advice Service & Labour Institutes) through the Inspectorates of Dock Safety located at major ports of India. Under the Dock Workers (Safety, Health and Welfare) Act, 1986 the Director General is the Chief Inspector of Dock Safety for all the major ports.

(8) Inter-State Migrant Workmen (Regulation of Employment and Conditions of Service) Act, 1979 : Section 16 of the Act stipulates that every contractor employing inter-state migrant workmen in connection with the work of an establishment to which this Act applies will have to provide the following facilities :

(a)   To ensure regular payment of wages to such workmen (at least minimum wages have to be paid as fixed under the Minimum Wages Act, 1948).

(b)   To ensure equal pay for equal work irrespective of gender.

(c)   To ensure suitable conditions of work to such workmen having regard for the fact that they are required to work in a state different from their own state.

(d)   To provide and maintain suitable residential accommodation to such workers working during the period of their employment.

(e)   To provide the prescribed medical facilities to the workmen, free of charge.

(f)   To provide such protective clothing to the workmen as may be prescribed.

(g)   In case of fatal accident or serious bodily injury to any such workman, to report to the specified authorities of both the states and also the next of kin of the workman.

With regard to labour welfare, the Act contains the provisions for appointment of a Labour Welfare Officer and his duties so far as welfare of workers are concerned.

3.4.2 Non-Statutory Labour Welfare Amenities or Facilities

As stated earlier, labour welfare facilities are classified in India as statutory and non-statutory labour welfare facilities. Statutory welfare amenities/facilities/measures comprise all those provisions given in the labour legislations the observance of which is binding on the employers by the concerned Acts.

Non-statutory labour welfare activities concern those activities which are undertaken voluntarily by employers, trade unions and some social organisations involved in labour welfare amenities or activities. The various types of labour welfare activities undertaken by the employers and organisations voluntarily can be broadly categorised under the following heads. All of them are non-statutory labour welfare amenities.

(a) Educational Facilities : Educational facilities for the workers and their children are provided in the form of provision of schools, reading rooms, libraries, financial assistance etc.

The education to workers' families, especially to their children is essential as it is an investment in training the workforce of the future. The **Commission on Labour Welfare [CLW]** recommended that educational facilities should be made part and parcel of the labour welfare activities. Educational facilities are usually provided by the state and employers to the workers' children in the form of schools and colleges. Some employers provide transport if the schools are far away. Some employers reimburse the cost of textbooks and scholarships. Library facilities and reading rooms are also provided voluntarily by some employers and social organisations.

(b) Transport Facilities : The rapid growth of Industrial Estates and workshops outside the cities has made commuting a problem for workers. To commute means to travel regularly by a train, a bus, a car or so on to and from one's work. The fatigue of travel to and from work has a detrimental effect on attendance of workers. Hence, it is very essential to provide suitable transport services. The transport services are provided by the state and local bodies. However, it is found that many employers also provide transport facilities to their workers or grant conveyance allowance.

(c) Medical Facilities : Medical facilities are provided in varying degrees by large establishments to their workers either in their own hospitals or by making necessary arrangements with well established medical institutions. Cotton and Woollen Textile Mills, Indian Jute Mills Association, many units in cement industry, sugar industry etc. provide medical facilities in one way or the other. Medical facilities are provided to workers and their families in the form of suitable equipped first-aid centres, hospitals and the like for the treatment of diseases, accidents etc.

(d) Family Planning : Considering the importance of family planning, C.L.W. recommended that the family planning programme should be made part and parcel of the labour welfare activities. It also suggested that centres and State Governments family planning schemes should give recognition to fully equipped and properly staffed hospitals run by the employers. The National Commission on Labour [N.C.L] also suggested to boost up the family planning programme. Many employers and organisations participate actively in such schemes and programmes.

(e) Distress Relief and Cash Benefits : This is one of the non-statutory welfare benefits and some employers give more importance to these benefits. They are called exgratia payments in case of death of a worker, injuries caused to workmen, marriages etc. Many employers even make arrangements or give advances for festivals. For example, by creating staff welfare funds, many employers provide the grants for prolonged illness, funeral expenses, operations etc. The Indian Railways has created a benefit fund to help their employees. Workers' organisations have stressed the need for distress relief funds in all industries to help the workers to cope with sudden calamities. Most mines also have introduced distress Relief Scheme.

(f) Housing Facilities : Considering the importance of housing and necessity of improving housing conditions of industrial workers, the Indian Industrial Commission and Royal Commission suggested various measures in that respect. The Government of India put forth the Industrial Housing Scheme in 1948. Many employers made available housing facilities to their workers in the form of self-contained tenements with various facilities such as electricity, sanitation and running water supply.

(g) Grain Shop Facilities through Consumer Co-Operative Societies : These societies provide to their members foodgrains and other essential goods at fair and reasonable prices. Many employers voluntarily provide assistance to these activities by participating in share capital, providing loans and grants. Apart from these, a employer should make arrangements for accommodation for stores either free of rent or at a nominal rent.

(h) Recreational Facilities : These facilities are important as they provide an opportunity to workers to enjoy their lives and reduce fatigue. Such facilities are provided in the form of music, dance, drama, recreational halls and various cultural activities by employers for the well being of their workers.

- Many organisations are now imparting education to workers through film shows, distribution of literature, counselling etc. for the prevention of AIDS and to check the growing menace of AIDS.

- For maintaining health and physical fitness, many employers and organisations have launched programmes like Yoga, physical fitness exercises and so on.

The above list is not complete. Besides the above mentioned non-statutory labour welfare amenities, facilities, benefits, employers and organisations provide other amenities to workers considering their needs and suggestions made by CWL, NCL and so on.

3.5 ROLE AND APPROACH OF THE GOVERNMENT IN RESPECT OF LABOUR WELFARE AND HEALTH

Working conditions, health and safety of workers, labour welfare are very important from the view point of economic and industrial development of our India. Therefore, the labour welfare movement is necessary to improve the conditions of workers so that they can live a better life.

The origin of labour welfare activity in India goes back to 1837 when the British colonies started importing Indian labour and labour welfare activity was largely controlled by legislation. Many Acts such as the Apprentices Act of 1850, the Fatal Accidents Act of 1853, the Merchant Shipping Act of 1959 etc. were passed with the objective of helping poor workers. However, considerable improvement did not take place in the sphere of labour welfare.

There was a rapid increase in industrial activities during and after the First World War, leading to a considerable increase in the number of industrial workers. The number of factories and workers working in the factories increased enormously. Total number of factories increased from 2936 in 1914 to 11,613 in 1939 while the number of factory workers increased from 9,50,000 to 17,50,000 during that period. Therefore, the Government took initiative and actively promoted various labour welfare activities for workers in different industrial sectors.

After Independence, the labour welfare movement acquired new dimensions. Considering the positive role of labour welfare in increasing productivity and reducing industrial tensions and unrest, the Government seriously took its social responsibility to introduce measures to increase labour welfare, especially weaker sections of the population. The Government of India formulated suitable schemes and included them in the Five-year plans. In all the Five-year plans, various labour welfare activities have been covered.

In early 1960s ergonomic studies mainly focused on the design of machine controls, plant layout, manual handling of heavy workloads and aspects such as noise, vibration, ventilation, temperature etc. affecting the health of workers, began to be taken into consideration. Over the years, ergonomic studies have contributed immensely to make the work places not only safer than before but also convenient and productive. Ergonomics implies the scientific study of relationship between man and his working environment. It takes into consideration not only the physical environment in which workers work but also their tools, materials, ways and methods of doing work. In fact, it is connected with the physical, biological, mental and behavioural aspects of an individual which are then related to labour welfare.

Considering the recommendations suggested by ILO and other committees and commissions, the Government of India enacted protective provisions in different Acts e.g. the Factories Act 1948, the Plantations Act of 1951, the Mines Act of 1952 etc. The regulatory environment for occupational health and safely has been encompassed in labour and industrial legislations.

Thus, it can be said that the health and safety of the people at work has been the subject of legislation since long and the role and approach of the Government is positive in respect to labour welfare. The Government started declaring National Safety Awards to give recognition to good safety performance on the part of industrial undertakings and to stimulate and maintain the interest of both the managements and workers in accident prevention programmes. This is very good action on the part of the Government to increase and maintain industrial safety and labour welfare.

The Government set up the **Factory Advice Service, and Labour Institute, Mumbai** which performs various functions as an integral body to advice the government, industries and other interested organisations concerned with matters relating to safety health and welfare of factory workers.

The Government has also drawn up **"The National Programme for Co-ordinated Action Plan"** for controlling hazards and for the protection of occupational health and safety of workers in dangerous manufacturing processes.

The Indian economy is developing in which the role and participation is noteworthy. Apart from the legislative responsibility, the Government as an employer has a basic social responsibility to play the role of a model employer and to provide various welfare amenities to its employees. The Government of India and State Governments like Maharashtra have involved themselves in the pioneering work in the field of labour welfare. They have set up model welfare centres through which various facilities like housing and medical facilities, educational and creational facilities and so on are provided to employees and their dependents.

Some states have constituted a Welfare Fund for providing labour welfare facilities such as medical facilities, reading rooms and library facilities, games and sports, excursions, tours and holiday homes.

From the discussion done so far, we can come to the conclusion that the Government does not function only as a regulator but also as an employer so far as labour welfare amenities are concerned. It performs a positive role and makes all efforts for increasing labour welfare and safety.

3.6 VARIOUS AGENCIES FOR PROVIDING LABOUR WELFARE AMENITIES

There are various agencies performing functions and doing work in the field of labour welfare and health. These agencies are as under :

(a)   The Central Government and various State Governments.

(b)   Employers.

(c)   Labour Unions.

(d)   Municipal corporations, municipalities, panchayats i.e. local self government authorities.

(e)   Voluntary organisations engaged in the activities for social welfare or social service.

3.7 ROLE OF EMPLOYERS, TRADE UNIONS AND VOLUNTARY ORGANISATIONS IN PROVIDING LABOUR WELFARE AMENITIES

Employers are required to provide certain welfare amenities and health services as per the provisions of various labour welfare legislations. Some employers have done and are doing really praiseworthy work in the field of labour welfare. They consider their workers as an invaluable asset and do every possible thing for the betterment of their workers. They do not require legal provisions to provide welfare amenities for their workers. There are many employers who started various welfare activities that proved to be forerunners of labour welfare.

It has been realised that employers have a significant role to play in providing welfare facilities to their workers at their work place and outside the work place over and above what is laid down by law. In the past, the employer regarded welfare work as a non-economic investment and a barren liability. But at present it is found that there is change in the attitude of the employers and gradual extension of scope of extent of welfare measures partly through the statutory provisions and partly through the employers' realisation that labour welfare is an important activity and an important aspect of human relations.

Besides the statutory labour welfare amenities many employers provide various labour welfare amenities on their own such as housing, educational facilities, sport activities, medical facilities, employment to one of the dependents etc.

Trade unions are regarded as part and parcel of the industrial system. The main activities of trade unions are to ensure adequate wages, secure better conditions of work and employment; better treatment to workers from their employers and to protect the interest of workers who are their members. They create a fund through subscriptions for supporting their members during unemployment, sickness, and lockouts. They arrange legal assistance to workers if needed. They also make provisions for the education of workers and their families.

The welfare activities of trade unions/worker's organisations include :

1. Social cultural and recreational activities.

2. Welfare Centres/Workers' Institutes.

3. Vocational Guidance Services.

4. Consumer's/producer's Credit Co-operative societies.

5. Provision of transport facilities.

6. Civil defence and campaigns for national integration, communal harmony etc.

7. Organisation of welfare and recreational activities.

8. Health and family planning programmes.

9. Literacy, adult education and social education classes.

10. Workers' education and leadership training courses.

11. Safety education.

12. Building houses for workers.

13. National Savings Schemes.

14. To participate or campaign for civic/social services for members such as schooling of children.

From the above mentioned welfare activities of trade unions and workers' organisations, we come to know the role played by these organisations.

There are many voluntary organisations or voluntary social service agencies which are engaged in useful labour welfare work. The Seva Sadan Society, The Maternity and Infant Welfare Association, The Depressed Classes' Mission Society and Women Institute of Bengal are a few such organisations. The welfare activities of these organisations cover mass education, promotion of public health, organisation of recreation and sports for the working class, cultural activities and many more. No doubt, these organisations also play an important role in the field of labour welfare.

POINTS TO REMEMBER

1. Various Welfare Amenities Provided to Labour

   (a) Hygienic Facilities and Amenities in Respect of Sanitation

   (b) Shelters and Rest Rooms

   (c) Lunch Rooms

   (d) Crèche and Wash Rooms for the Children

   (e) Health Services and First-aid Appliances

   (f) Health Services in Respect of Dangerous Operations

(g) Facilities in Respect of Latrines, Urinals and Spittoons

(h) Transport Facilities

(i) Educational Facilities

(j) Medical Facilities

(k) Housing Facilities

(l) Recreational Facilities

(m) Cooperative Societies

2. **Statutory Labour Welfare Amenities**

(1) The Factories Act of 1948

(2) The Mines Act, 1952 and the Mines Rules

(3) The Plantations Labour Act, 1951

(4) The Motor Transport Workers Act, 1961

(5) The Contract Labour (Regulation and Abolition) Act, 1970

(6) The Merchant Shipping Act, 1958

(7) Dock Workers (Safety, Health and Welfare) Scheme, 1961

(8) Inter-State Migrant Workmen (Regulation of Employment and Conditions of Service) Act, 1979

3. **Non-Statutory Labour Welfare Amenities or Facilities**

(a) Educational Facilities

(b) Transport Facilities

(c) Medical Facilities

(d) Family Planning

(e) Distress Relief and Cash Benefits

(f) Housing Facilities

(g) Grain Shop Facilities through Consumer Co-operative Societies

(h) Recreational Facilities

QUESTIONS FOR DISCUSSION

Q.1   Describe various welfare amenities provided to labour.

Q.2   Classify the labour welfare amenities.

Q.3   Explain various statutory welfare amenities. What role does the government play in that respect?

Q.4   What are non-statutory welfare amenities? Which agencies participate in providing non-statutory welfare amenities?

Q.5   Explain the role of employers, government and trade unions in providing labour welfare amenities.

Q.6   Explain the importance of labour welfare work.

Q.7   Write notes on the following :

   (a)   Classification of labour welfare amenities.

   (b)   Non-statutory labour welfare amenities.

   (c)   Statutory labour welfare amenities.

   (d)   Agencies providing labour welfare amenities.

   (e)   Role of the government in respect of labour welfare and health.

QUESTIONS FROM PREVIOUS EXAMINATIONS

Q.1   Explain the role of Trade Unions and management towards the welfare of employees in Industrial Organisations.   **[April-2013]**

Q.2   Explain the Welfare provisions under Factories Act.   **[April-2007]**

Q.3   What are the provisions of Factories Act relating to Welfare of Workers?

                                                                      [Dec-2007]

Q.4   Describe the Welfare and Health Provisions under the Factories Act. 1948.

                                                                      [April-2009]

Q.5   Explain the Role of Trade Unions towards the Welfare of Employees.   **[April-2009]**

Q.6   "Trade Unions aim at Securing economic security and labour welfare activities." Explain the Statement with Justification.   **[April-2010]**

Q.7   State the Statutory Welfare, Safety and Health Provisions under the Factories Act. 1948.   **[Dec-2010, April-2011]**

Q.8   Critically Examine Labour Welfare Measures undertaken by the Government.

                                                                      [April-2011]

Q.9   Write Short Notes on :

   (a)   Role of Government in Labour Welfare.   **[April-2010]**

   (b)   Crèche.   **[Dec-2010]**

                                ✍ ✍ ✍

Chapter 4...

Workers' Education Scheme and Workers' Participation in Management

Contents ...

Learning Objectives

At the end of the chapter, you will understand :

- Meaning and objectives of workers' education and rationale behind workers' education scheme
- Workers' education scheme in India and its objectives
- Constitution and functions of the C.B.W.E
- Meaning of workers' participation in management
- Pre-requisites for successful working of workers' participation in management
- Various objectives of workers' participation in management
- Methods of workers' participation in management
- Levels of workers' participation in management
- Advantages of workers' participation in management

4.1 INTRODUCTION

Education of workers and workers' participation in management are important for motivating the workers to enhance self confidence and building up of morale amongst them. Workers' education scheme helps the workers to equip for their intellectual participation in social and economic development.

Workers' education helps workers to increase their productivity and efficiency and it ultimately leads to increase in their welfare. Workers' participation in management is considered as a mechanism where workers have a say in the decision making process of their enterprises. The workers' participation schemes, if implemented properly, lead to the achievement of security of employment, better wages, bonus etc. This is all related to the welfare aspect of labour. In this chapter, let us study important aspects related to workers' education scheme and workers' participation in management.

4.2 MEANING OF WORKERS' EDUCATION AND RATIONALE BEHIND WORKERS' EDUCATION SCHEME IN INDIA

The term **"Workers' Education"** simply means *providing necessary knowledge, information, training to workers considering the nature of work they perform so that their skills, efficiency, productivity can be increased.*

Workers' education is expected to contribute to the harmonious development of workers' personality, their role in the society and knowledge, aptitudes and attitudes required for such roles. It emphasises group advancement as well as solution to group problems. From this point of view, workers' education attempts to provide workers better understanding of their role, status, rights and duties, responsibilities. Workers' education lays more stress on group advancement. It differs from traditional, vocational and professional education because traditional, vocational and professional education is meant for individual advancement and progress.

It may be noted that the term workers' education is interpreted variously in different countries because of historical reasons. In the U.S.A., it implies training to trade union leadership. It covers trade unionism, general audit education and vocational education in the U.K. This term workers' education is used in a wider connotation in developing countries like India and it aims at making the workers better operators, better union members and better citizens. One of the important objectives of workers' education is the development of human resources.

After India gained independence, she took up the task of rebuilding her economy. At that stage it was considered necessary to educate the Indian workers. The Indian Constitution laid emphasis on the need for an effective programme of education for all individuals, especially for a large percentage of the labour force; which is drawn from rural areas and is mostly literate.

One of the important factors which led to the introduction of Workers' Education Scheme in India was the high rate of illiteracy among the masses. According to the census of 1951, about 70% of the total population was illiterate. The illiteracy rate of Indian workers was unduly high. This, in fact led to the formulation of the Workers' Education Scheme in India. The government of India appointed an international committee of experts in co-operation with the Ford Foundation for advice on the scheme. The committee submitted its report in March 1957. On the basis of the report of the committee and its recommendations the Central Board of Workers' Education was set up in 1958 to administer and implement the workers' education scheme. Thus, for the success of industrialisation, economic development, and labour welfare, the workers' education scheme was taken up and the Central Board for Workers' Education was constituted by the government of India to implement and administer the workers' education scheme.

4.2.1 Definitions and Nature of Workers' Education

Workers' education is one of the key objectives of the **Ministry of Labour and Employment**. In order to achieve this objective, various educational schemes and programmes are implemented. From the following definitions of workers' education, we come to know the meaning, importance and the important objectives of workers' education.

(a) According to **Florence Peterson**, *"Workers' education is not a generic term but it has a specific connotation. It is a special kind of adult education designed to give workers a better understanding for their status, problems, rights and responsibilities as workers, as union members, as consumers and as citizens".*

(b) **Harry Laidlaw** opined that, *"Workers' education is an attempt on the part of organised labour to educate his own members under an educational system in which the workers prescribe the courses of instructions, select the teachers and in considerable measure furnish finance".*

(c) In the **Encyclopaedia of Social Sciences**, the comprehensive definition of workers' education is given. It is stated, *"Workers' participation seeks to help the worker to solve his problems not as an individual but as a member of his social class as a whole. Workers' education has to take into consideration the educational needs of the workers as an individual for his personal evolution; as an operative - for his efficiency and advancement, as a citizen for a happy and integrated life in community; as a member of a trade union – for the protection of his interests as a member of working class".*

From the above mentioned definitions of workers' education, we came to know that workers' education is important for the overall development of workers. It is also adult education and includes various schemes, programmes etc. which help to increase the understanding of workers and also efficiency and productivity. Ultimately, it leads to increase in the welfare of labour.

4.2.2 Objectives of Workers' Education

The National Commission on Labour, the Workers' Education Review Committee, India and other experts have suggested various objectives of workers' education.

Some of the important objectives of workers' education are as follows :

(a) To assist workers to acquire skills, knowledge, attitudes etc. necessary for collective work performance.

(b) To enhance existing knowledge and performance capabilities of workers.

(c) To bring skills, capabilities of workers up to a standard for the present and future job assignments.

(d) To increase the efficiency, competency, and productivity of workers.

(e) To develop stronger and more effective trade unions through better wel trained officials and more enlightened members for strengthening the bonds of loyalty to the trade unions.

(f) To equip the workers to take its place in democratic society and to fulfil ts social and economic responsibilities.

(g) To promote among workers a greater and proper understanding of the problems of their economic environment and their privileges and obligations as the members of their trade unions.

(h) To make the worker a responsible, committed and well disciplined operative.

(i) To lead workers to a clean and healthy life based on a firm ethical foundation.

(j) To create matured and sensible leadership through the rank to lead trade union movement in a proper and meaningful way.

(k) To achieve the purpose of life and raise the workers to elevate themselves to a sense of achievement.

4.3 WORKERS' EDUCATION SCHEME IN INDIA

The workers' education programme is of recent origin. In cooperation with the Ford Foundation, the government of India appointed an International Committee of Experts for providing advice on the workers' education scheme. The committee submitted its report in March 1957. On the basis of the recommendations of that committee, a tripartite semi-autonomous body known as "The Central Board for Workers' Education" [C.B.W.E.] was constituted in 1958 under the Ministry of Labour, Government of India, to formulate policies and programmes, to administer and to implement the Workers' Education Scheme.

The C.B.W.E. established the Indian Institute of Workers' Education in 1970 to conduct training programmes at the national level for its officials and trade union leaders. This institution serves as an Apex level demonstration and training institute. The institute organises and conducts training programmes and refresher courses for educating the officers, courses for trade union functionaries and also provides library and allied services.

The C.B.W.E. conducts long-term and short-term programmes of training for the industrial workers and rural educators through its regional and sub-regional centres. The regional and sub-region as centres have been opened to conduct educational activities in important industrial centres or areas.

4.3.1 Important Objectives of the Workers' Education Scheme

The Workers' Education Scheme is framed to achieve certain objectives. The most important objective is to develop the human resources properly. The other objectives are as follows :

(a) To develop stronger and effective trade unions, to strengthen the democratic process and traditions in trade union movement through better trained officials and enlightened members.

(b) To equip all workers for their participation in social and economic development of our country for establishing a democratic society and to fulfil their social and economic responsibilities.

(c) To promote among workers proper understanding of the problems of their economic and social environment, their responsibilities towards their family members, their rights, duties and liabilities as citizens, as workers in industry and trade unions.

(d) To develop quality leadership from the rank and file of the workers themselves and to promote the growth of the democratic process and trade union organisation and administration.

(e) To enable the trade unions themselves to take over the functions of workers' education ultimately.

(f) To enhance self-confidence to motivate for family welfare planning and to combat social evils.

4.3.2 Nature of Training Programmes for Workers' Education

The Central Board of Workers' Education [CBWE] has developed a need based programme for educating the workers, worker teachers and education officers. It is a three-tier training programme.

In the first stage, education officers in the service of the CBWE are trained. The period of training is generally for four months full-time after which they are employed in the services of the CBWE and later they are posted at different regional centres. Nominees of different trade unions are also admitted to this course so that they can also undertake workers' education programmes under the auspices of their trade unions.

At the second stage of the programme, the workers in selected numbers are trained as 'Worker Teachers' at the regional and sub-regional centres by the education officers. The worker teachers' course of training is continuous full-time course of the duration of three months. It is conducted in batches of about 20 to 30 number of workers.

The selection of worker, teacher training is made by the Regional Advisory Committee attached to every regional centre. The trainees selected are sponsored by the trade unions. Such trainees are released by the related employers with full wages for the full duration of the training. The syllabus covers various topics on trade unionism, union and management relations, economics for trade-unionists, labour laws, labour welfare, workers' education etc.

The third stage starts when the worker teachers complete their training at the regional centres and go back to their factories or establishments or places of work. They conduct training programmes for the rank and file workers in the unit level classes. The duration of the unit level class is of three months and largely outside the working hours. Generally accommodations, furniture and various other facilities are provided by the management for conducting the classes. Some managements give time-off to workers for attending the unit level classes. Full-time unit level classes of the duration of three weeks are also organised where necessary facilities for conducting the classes are available. For giving training, the whole syllabus is grouped under various headings, e.g. workers and the industry, workers and the trade unions, etc.

The C.B.W.E. also conducts, in addition to this, special short-term training programmes, correspondence courses and provides financial assistance in the form of grant-in-aid to encourage trade unions to undertake workers' education programmes themselves. Training programmes are conducted for members of works committees, joint management councils and officials of trade unions.

Three day seminars, study circles, refresher courses etc. are organised for worker teachers and worker trainees. Besides these programmes, special courses on population education, participative education, trade union education, productivity education are also conducted at different levels.

Some central trade union organisations have set up agencies to promote educational activities for workers and for trade union leaders, e.g. the INTUC set up "Central Institute of Workers' Education in 1972 for Workers' Education".

In the beginning, the C.B.W.E. concentrated its training activities in the organised sector, but it shifted its emphasis to rural sector since 177-78 on the recommendations of the Workers' Education Review Committee. The C.B.W.E. initially started with seven pilot projects. Now it has become a regular and continuing programme.

The C.B.W.E. also organises tailor-made programmes considering the functional and educational needs of the workers from power-loom, handloom, khadi and village industries, small scale units, handicrafts, coir industry, bidi industry, workers of weaker section such as handicapped workers, women workers, rickshaw drivers etc. The C.B.W.E. conducts special full-time two months' programme for rural workers to educate them considering their needs. On 2nd October, 1978, C.B.W.E launched an adult education programme to cater to the needs of illiterate workers in traditional industries, mines, plantations and in rural areas.

The C.B.W.E. has undertaken the responsibility to implement the new scheme under the Mahatma Gandhi National Rural Employment Guarantee Act [MGNREGA] from 2011-12. The special programmes for the beneficiaries are conducted by the C.B.W.E. through its Regional Directorates to enlighten rural masses the benefits under the MGNREGA and its schemes.

4.4 CONSTITUTION AND FUNCTIONS OF THE CENTRAL BOARD FOR WORKERS' EDUCATION [C.B.W.E]

Workers' education programmes are sponsored by the government of India and are administered through the C.B.W.E. The C.B.W.E. is the semi-autonomous body and was constituted in 1958 under the Ministry of Labour and Employment, Government of India. The C.B.W.E. has been registered under the Society's Registration Act of 1860. This semi-autonomous body is entrusted with the task of framing its policies, allocating funds, and also overseeing the proper and effective execution of its policies.

Constitutionally, the maximum number of members of the C.B.W.E. is twenty. They are as follows :

(a)   A chairman nominated by the government of India.

(b)   Representatives of the Central as well as State governments.

(c)   Representatives of the trade unions, organisations of the employers and educational institutions nominated by the Government of India.

(d)   One trade unionist to be nominated by the Ministry of Labour.

(e)   Apart from the Chairman, there is a Director appointed by the Government of India.

He is entrusted with the duties to plan and implement the policies of the C.B.W.E. There is the Board of Governors which manages and controls the affairs of the C.B.W.E. It is also responsible for the managerial and administrative activities of the board. This body is headed by the President and it is composed of two Vice-presidents, a Secretary and other members who represent the government, employers and labour totalling not more than ten members.

The headquarters of the C.B.W.E. is in Nagpur where the office of the director is situated. The C.B.W.E. has its own training institute at Mumbai.

The Indian Institute of Workers' Education, Mumbai, the Regional Centres, the Sub-Regional Centres and the unit-level classes are below the head office of the C.B.W.E. in the organisational set-up.

Through its network of more than 50 regional and 10 sub-regional centres, the C.B.W.E. conducts long-term and short-term programmes for the industrial workers and rural educators. The regional level activities are monitored and supervised by the four offices which are located at Delhi, Kolkata, Chennai, and Mumbai. A regional advisory committee has been constituted for each regional centre to review the programmes of the workers' education scheme in the region and also to recommend suitable and proper measures for effective implementation of the programme.

The Indian Institute of Workers' Education has been established by the C.B.W.E. in 1970 to conduct various training programmes at national levels for its officials and trade union leaders. This institution serves as an Apex level demonstration and training institute. It organises and conducts training programmes as well as refresher courses for education officers, courses for trade union functionaries, and provides library and allied services.

4.4.1 Functions of the C.B.W.E.

As workers' education aims at achieving various objectives such as creating and increasing awareness and sense of responsibility, effective participation of the workers in the socio-economic development of the country to promote the growth of democratic process and trade union organisation and administration, to help to increase the efficiency and productivity of workers etc. Training programmes, seminars are organised by the C.B.W.E. for the workers working in urban and rural areas, informal and informal sectors at national, regional and unit levels through a network of more than 50 regional and sub-regional directorates spread all over the country.

For administering and implementing the workers' education scheme, the C.B.W.E. performs various functions. Important functions of the C.B.W.E. are mentioned below :

(a) To administer and implement the workers' education scheme.

(b) To establish regional centres in different regions.

(c) To train the education officers and worker teachers.

(d) To frame syllabi and prepare study material in the form of pamphlets, books, charts etc. in order to make training effective.

(e) To encourage the organisations of employers as well as of workers to promote and develop their own workers' education schemes.

(f) To arrange various programmes for instruction on trade union consciousness.

(g) To evaluate the progress of the workers' education schemes and to introduce necessary measures to correct deficiencies in the scheme in order to make the schemes more effective.

(h) To make whole hearted efforts to strengthen among all sections of working class a sense of patriotism, the feeling of national integrity, unity, amity (i.e. friendshipness), communal harmony and pride in being an Indian.

(i) To develop capacity of workers in all aspects to meet the challenges of the country from time to time.

4.4.2 The C.B.W.E. and its Regional Centres

The C.B.W.E. is empowered to set-up regional centres and local committees to look after the working of the centres. The regional centres are headed by the regional directors. The local committees consist of representatives of the Government of India, trade unions, organisations of employees and also of the educational institutions. These local committees appoint sub-committees. Certain functions are entrusted to the sub-committees appointed by the local committees.

At all the regional centres, two types of sub-committees are constituted and they are Selection sub-committee and Syllabus sub-committee. The selection sub-committee takes part in selecting the candidates for the worker teacher training courses. The syllabus sub-committee undertakes the responsibility of reviewing various syllabi framed for the training courses at the unit level. This committee also suggests the changes in the syllabi according to the needs periodically.

4.4.3 Finances Provided to the C.B.W.E. and its Expenditure

The main source of finance to the C.B.W.E. is the grants received from the Ministry of Labour and Employment. Finance is obviously required for running the workers' education programmes. Though there are a few other sources of finance, their share is negligible and they add up to only one percent of the total income of the C.B.W.E.

The C.B.W.E.'s expenditure is incurred at three levels – the head office, the regional office and at unit levels. The major expenses are incurred in the administration of the scheme and running the programmes. The stipends as per rules are paid to the trainees who attend the training courses of education officers. The head office expenditure is mainly on establishment, salaries, honorarium, allowances etc.

The expenditure at the regional level is of two types. One relating to administration and the other is related to the implementation of the workers' education scheme.

Expenditure is also incurred at the unit level. Such expenditure includes the fees paid to worker-teachers, money spent on local excursions, costs paid as incentive awards.

4.5 WORKERS' PARTICIPATION IN MANAGEMENT

Management is the process of designing and maintaining an environment in which individuals employed in an organisation, working together in groups effectively and efficiently, make all efforts to accomplish the selected goals or objectives. As managers and the concerned employees carry out management functions of planning, production, organising, staffing, leading, controlling etc. there must be proper coordination. For performing these functions, there must be healthy industrial relations between management and workers.

In fact, an industrial relation system involves three parties i.e. management, workers and government. Management and workers are the two direct parties. Government is the third party which plays an indirect role in maintaining good and healthy industrial relations by implementing suitable policies and providing legal framework. Good industrial relations between management and workers means that they settle their differences through mutual consultations and proper decisions. Workers' participation is also known as **labour** or **employee participation**. The concept of workers' participation in management is considered as a mechanism in which workers have a say in the decision-making process of their organisation.

4.6 DEFINITIONS AND MEANING OF THE CONCEPT OF WORKERS' PARTICIPATION

The concept of workers' participation in management has been a vague and debatable issue in the field of industrial relations and hence, it has acquired different meanings for different people. It is difficult to define the concept of workers' participation very clearly because it is associated with varying practices in different countries, its content and form being in accordance with the socio-economic objectives of a country. However, it seems that the concept of workers' participation in management has its roots in the human relations movement in the domain of industrial organisations. The humanitarian approach to labour has brought about a new set of values for labour and management.

According to **Johannes Schregle**, *"Workers participation is based on the fundamental concept that the ordinary worker invests his labour in and ties his fate to his place of work and that, therefore, he has a legitimate right to have a share in influencing the various aspects to company policy"*.

But there are other experts who have different views about workers' participation in management. It is observed that some management people argue that those who take risks should have the right to take necessary decisions about managing their organisations. Hence, they have every right to formulate the goals, the policies relating to organisational activities and do not like any encroachment on it. Despite the different views, generally, it is agreed that workers' participation in management is an essential step which involves redistribution of power between management and workers in the direction of industrial democracy. In fact, the concept of industrial democracy is based on the concept of workers' participation in management.

Industrial democracy is generally defined as *'a programme of government mandated workers' participation at various levels of organisation with regard to the decisions which affect the workers'*. Sometimes, the concept of industrial democracy is also applied to voluntary programmes besides the mandated ones. Let us consider some important definitions of workers' participation in management in order to understand the concept of workers' participation in management.

(1) Keith Davis : *"Workers' participation in management is the mental and emotional involvement of a person in a group which encourages him to contribute the goals and share responsibilities in them"*.

(2) C. B. Memoria : *"Workers' participation in management is a system of communication and consultation either in a formal or informal way by which employees of an organisation are kept informed about the affairs of the undertaking and through which they express their opinion and contribute to management decisions"*.

(3) International Labour Organisation [ILO] : *"Workers' participation may, broadly, be taken to cover all terms of association of workers and their representatives with the decision-making process, ranging from exchanging of information, consultations, decisions and negotiations to more institutionalised forms such as the presence of workers' members on management or supervisory boards or even management by workers themselves as practised in Yugoslavia".*

Workers' participation in management is governed by the Law on Workers' Management of State Economic Enterprises and Higher Economic Association in Yugoslavia. That Act has prescribed three-tier participation structure which consists of collective, workers' council and board of management. The collective holds referenda and periodical meetings in order to know the opinions of workers on various issues, matters etc.

The workers' council is an elected body by the collective. It takes various decisions on labour relations, discipline, productivity, remuneration, health, safety, etc. The board of management is entrusted overall management of an enterprise and at least seventy five percent of its members are from workers who are directly engaged in production. Of course, it is obvious that this system of workers' participation in management is not found in other countries. Hence, there can be different views about workers' participation in management and arrangements also.

(4) McGregor Douglas : *"The term workers' participation implies a formal method of providing an opportunity for every member of the organisation to contribute his brain and ingenuity as well as his physical efforts to the improvement of organisational effectiveness".*

Though there are various definitions stated by the authorities on the subject and different views about workers' participation in management, it is certain that the concept of workers' participation in management generally implies the association or participation of workers management without final authority and responsibility in the decision-making process. It gives a higher status to workers without treating them merely as wage-earners. It can be said that the important purpose behind it is to create cordial labour-management relations and to avoid industrial unrest and disputes.

4.7 PRE-REQUISITES FOR SUCCESSFUL WORKING OF WORKERS' PARTICIPATION IN MANAGEMENT

It is needless to say that workers' participation in management, besides other things, provides a better status to workers and helps to create industrial democracy. It also makes workers more responsible and responsive to the needs of their organisation. Moreover, it creates a feeling of involvement among workers and it acts as a bridge between the management and workers. Hence, it is very essential to create a suitable atmosphere for making the workers' participation in management successful. Below are given some of the important pre-requisites or conditions for the successful functioning of workers' participation schemes in management.

(a) The attitude of an organisation/management should be constructive and progressive. It must sincerely and whole heartedly accept the concept of workers' participation and must be prepared to give a fair trial to the schemes of workers' participation.

(b) Both parties should have genuine faith, mutual trust in the system and in each other. Moreover, they must be willing to work together.

(c) There should be progressive management and it should recognise its obligations, responsibilities etc. towards their unions.

(d) Trade union must be strong and democratic with a genuine and prudent leadership. The union leaders should have genuine desire to participate in the management. The attitude of union leaders should be positive, cooperative and not aggressive.

(e) There should be closely and mutually formulated objectives for successful participation by management as well as trade unions.

(f) There should be effective two-way communication for making the workers' participation successful. For that purpose, frequent meetings of representatives of workers and their employers/management should be held to discuss various issues relating to workers' participation schemes and to conduct negotiations for the solution of pending problems. Both the parties should make all the efforts to develop a favourable attitude towards the schemes of participative management.

(g) Workers should be given proper education and training as regards the schemes of workers participation. Along with workers, supervisory staff should also be associated with the management.

(h) The follow-up actions on the decisions of the participating forums should be ensured.

(i) There should be full recognition of the rights and claims of both the parties. Workers should no doubt be conscious of their rights, but at the same time, emphasis must also be laid on their responsibilities.

(j) Workers' participation in the management cannot be effective unless the state of labour-management relations in the organisation is healthy. Besides this, workers' participation in management cannot be effective unless the state of labour-management relations in the organisation is healthy. Besides this, workers' participation in management cannot be effective unless there is an adequate machinery for collective bargaining.

4.8 OBJECTIVES OF WORKERS' PARTICIPATION IN MANAGEMENT

Workers' participation in management is considered as a means of self-realisation in work. Further, it helps to meet the psychological needs of workers at work by eliminating to a large extent the feeling of futility, isolation and consequent frustration that they face in a normal industrial setting.

The objectives of workers' participation in management may vary from country to country because socio-economic development, political philosophy, industrial relations scene, attitudes of working class and of trade unions are different. However, the objectives of workers' participation in management which are considered as very important are mentioned below :

(a) To develop good industrial relations.

(b) To create and increase better understanding among the workers about their role and place in the process of attainment of organisational goals and objectives.

(c) To stimulate workers for higher productivity for the benefits of themselves for the advantage of their organisations and society at large.

(d) To satisfy the workers' social and esteem needs.

(e) To create among the workers the feeling of dignity and self-respect.

(f) To strengthen labour-management co-operation for maintaining industrial peace and harmony.

(g) To establish industrial democracy.

(h) To avoid external interference.

(i) To build dynamic human resources systematically.

(j) To share financial and other information about the organisation for the purpose of collective bargaining.

4.9 FORMS OR METHODS OF WORKERS' PARTICIPATION IN MANAGEMENT

The forms or methods in which workers can participate in management vary, depending upon the pattern of management, levels of management, size of the factory, authority delegated to subordinates, areas in which participation is sought etc. Certain methods are specified by the legal framework while certain methods are evolved in the process. In India some methods have been prescribed by law while many other methods have been suggested through guidelines formulated by the Government.

When workers participate in management either though a formal mechanism or through informal procedures, it is considered as an instance of participative management. For this effective functioning, both the parties i.e. labour and management must be keenly interested.

It is obvious that management interest basically lies in reducing cost and in improving the productivity.

On the other hand, workers are interested in increasing their earnings and to get various facilities. When earnings increase through sharing gains in productivity, a harmony of interests can be promoted. Hence, if participation is to be made effective and successful as a process or device, it should be integrated properly with a scheme of improving productivity as well as gain sharing.

Participation can be ascending participation or descending participation. In ascending participation, workers are given an opportunity to influence managerial decisions at higher levels through their elected representatives. While in descending participation, workers may be given more powers to plan and make decisions about their work.

The Important Forms or Methods of Workers' Participation in Management :

(a) **Works Committee :** A works committee is a forum provided under the Industrial Disputes Act of 1947 for explaining the difficulties of the parties concerned with the disputes. It endeavours to maintain cordial relationships even though there are disputes or differences between the parties to the disputes. The success of work committees mainly depends on the efforts and cooperation of both the parties to the disputes.

Section 3 (1) of this Act provides for a Works Committee. According to this section, in the case of any industrial establishment in which one hundred or more workmen are employed or have been employed on any day in the preceding twelve months, the appropriate Government may by general or special order require the employer to constitute in the prescribed manner a Works Committee consisting of representatives of employers and workmen engaged in the establishment.

However, the number of representatives of workmen on the committee shall not be less than the number of representatives of the employer. The representatives of the workmen shall be chosen in the prescribed manner from among the workmen engaged in the establishment and in consultation with their trade union, if any, registered under the Indian Trade Unions Act, 1926.

Section 3 (2) further provides that it shall be the duty of the Works Committee to promote measures for securing and preserving amity and good relations between the employer and workmen and, to that end to comment upon matters of their common interest or concern and endeavour to compose any material difference of opinion in respect of such matters.

Industrial Disputes Act, 1947 promotes the settlement of industrial disputes firstly by voluntary negotiations. Works Committees make prominent efforts towards that goal. Works Committees are joint committees having equal number of representatives of employers and workmen. The constitution of Works Committee is a must in an industrial establishment wherein one hundred or more workmen are employed on any day in the preceding twelve months. Works Committee is an internal media for settlement of Industrial Disputes Act within the industry.

Sub-Section 2 of **Section 3** of this Act enumerates the duties or functions of a Works Committee which are as follows :

(i)   To remove the disparities between employers and workmen.

(ii) To promote measures for securing and preserving amity, and friendly and good relations between the employers and workmen.

(iii) To that end, to comment upon all matters of their common interest or concern.

(iv) To make efforts to compose any material difference of opinion in respect of various matters. These matters include many aspects such as welfare of workers, provision and supervision of various recreational facilities, training of workmen and their wages, bonus, gratuity, working conditions including discipline, promotions, transfers etc. Thus, it seems that there is no subject concerning the relation between the employers and workmen which the Works Committee is precluded from considering. However, the following points must be remembered in this connection.

1.   Findings of the Works Committee are advisory or recommendatory and not mandatory. It cannot decide and pass final judgement. Its duty is only to comment because it is mainly a negotiating organ. It is the function of the Works Committee to promote measures for harmonious, friendly and good relations between the employers and workmen.

2.   Works Committees are not intended to supersede or supplement the trade unions for the purpose of collective bargaining. They are not authorised to consider real changes or substantial changes in the service conditions. They are not a substitute of trade unions.

The success of a works committee mainly depends upon :

(a)   The responsible and positive attitude on the part of management and,

(b)   The wholehearted implementation of its recommendations.

Being a legal provision, works committees have been constituted in most organisations.

(b) Joint Management Councils : A Joint Management Council (JMC) consists of representatives of management and workers. The J. M. Council performs advisory role on various matters specified. The J. M. Council is expected to be consulted on matters relating to the administration of standing orders, welfare measures, rationalisation, retrenchment etc.

The important functions performed by a J. M. Council are as follows :

(i)   J.M.C. is to be consulted by the management on the matters like standing orders, rationalisation, retrenchment, closure, reduction of operations.

(ii)   To receive information, to discuss and offer suggestions on general economic situations, market position, production and marketing programmes, methods of production, long-term capital budgeting decisions, modernisation, development and growth etc.

(iii) To shoulder administrative responsibilities like maintaining welfare measures, safety measures, training schemes and programmes, payment of rewards, scheduling of working hours, problems of indiscipline, absenteeism etc. J. M. Council takes up and suggests the measures in respect of the matters mentioned above.

It should be noted that J. M. Council merely performs the advisory role on the matter specified and its recommendations are not accepted as a mandatory requirement. Further, various matters which are likely to be sorted out through collective bargaining such as wages, bonus etc. are kept out of its purview. Similarly, it does not deal with the personal problems of an individual worker.

In India, a large number of J. M. Councils are established. However, the real contribution of the councils is limited.

The important reasons of the limited success of the J. M. Councils are as follows :

(i)   Trade unions generally oppose such councils as the trade unions feel that their importance may be reduced in the course of time. Hence, their attitude towards the J. M. Council becomes negative.

(ii)   The attitude of employers or managements of the organisations is not progressive and favourable for the effective working of the J. M. Councils.

(c) Workers' Participation on the Board of Directors : Appointments of employees' or workers' representatives on the Board of Directors is an important form or method of workers' participation in management. The basic idea behind this method is that the workers' representation of the Board of Directors' Level may help to establish industrial democracy and to create and maintain better employer-employee relations. As workers' representatives are appointed on the Board of Directors, it is expected that they would make all the efforts to protect the interests of their workers.

Under this method, the representatives are either elected or nominated, may be two or three, by the workers who attend the meeting of the Board and participate in their deliberations. The representatives of workers on the Board of Directors make all the efforts to bring to the notice of other directors the views, problems etc. of the workers and give suggestions. Thus, they participate in the process of problem solving and decision-making at the top level. However, this method is not very effective in bridging the gap between workers and their management because of the following important reasons :

(i)   As the workers' representatives are in minority they cannot bring any pressure on the other Directors. As a result, suggestion of the representatives of workers are not given proper or due attention and the gap between the two parties continue.

(ii) The Board meetings are held mainly to discuss managerial problems and not the problems of workers. Naturally, the workers' representatives get limited opportunities to discuss views, problems etc. of the workers.

(iii) Decision-making process at the board level is rather complex, complicated which requires specific skills than alternative form of participation for which workers' representatives neither possess skills nor do they have mental set.

(iv) There are rival trade unions. Naturally, workers' representatives appointed on the Board cannot put forward the views, problems, suggestions which are acceptable to all the workers. Moreover, participation at the board level weakens the bargaining power of trade unions as they have to accept the decisions of the Board having their own representatives.

(d) Suggestion Scheme : Under this scheme, workers are associated with the management through their suggestions on various matters relating to their working. A suggestion committee or suggestion screening committee is constituted with equal representation from management and workers. Workers are encouraged to give their suggestions to the management. The committee constituted for that purpose screens and evaluates the suggestions received from workers. The suggestions are accepted if they are found suitable and useful. Rewards are also given to those workers who give constructive suggestions for the benefit of all. Suggestion boxes are kept at convenient places in some organisations. The suggestions also can be given to a joint committee of workers and management or to the departmental heads.

(e) Shop Councils : A shop council is a method or a form of workers' participation in management wherein for each department or a shop in a unit, a shop council is constituted. Each shop council consists of an equal number of representatives of employers and workers. The employers' representatives are nominated by the management. All such representatives are nominated from within the unit concerned. The workers' representatives are obviously from among the workers of their department or shop concerned.

The number of members of each shop council is determined by the employers in consultation with the recognised trade union. Generally, the total number of a shop council does not exceed twelve. Various decisions of a shop council are arrived at on the basis of consensus and not by the process of voting.

A shop council works for a minimum period of two years. In other words, the tenure of a shop council is for a period of two years. This method of workers' participation was launched in India in 1975.

The important functions of shop councils are as follows

(i) To assist the management in achieving production targets.

(ii) To take necessary steps to improve productivity, efficiency and to increase production to the optimum.

(iii) To eliminate wastage and to make all efforts to utilise manpower and machine capacity effectively.

(iv) To recommend various steps to reduce absenteeism in the shop or department considering the causes of absenteeism.

(v) To make suggestions for providing safety measures.

(vi) To assist and maintain general discipline in the shop or department.

(vii) To provide various welfare measures for efficient running of the shop or department.

(viii) To make all efforts to provide various physical facilities such as lighting, ventilation, dust control, noise control etc.

(ix) To ensure proper flow of adequate two-way communication between the management and the workers for efficient working of the shop or department.

(f) Joint Councils : There is a participation of management and of workers in the Joint Councils. These councils work for the whole unit and their membership remains confined to those who are actually engaged in the organisation. The tenure of the Joint Councils is for two years.

The Chief Executive of the unit works as the Chairman and workers' members of the council nominate the Vice-chairman. The Secretary is appointed by the Joint Council.

The Joint Councils meet once in four months, but the periodicity of the meeting varies from unit to unit, it may be once in a month, quarter etc.

The decisions are taken in the Joint Council meeting by the process of consensus and the management implements the discussions within one month.

Under the 20-Point Economic Programme, factories employing five hundred or more workers constituted Joint Councils.

The important functions performed by Joint Councils from which their nature becomes clear are as follow :

(i) To increase the output by fixation of standards.

(ii) To consider various matters which could not be solved by shop councils.

(iii) To make all efforts to develop the skills of workers by providing them necessary and adequate training facilities.

(iv) To encourage employees for research and to give awards to workers involving creative work.

(v) To prepare a schedule of working laws.

(vi) To ensure full and proper utilisation of finished goods.

(vii) To provide general health, welfare and safety measures for the unit of the plant.

(g) Unit Councils : The scheme of workers' participation was launched in 1977 in commercial and service organisations in the public sector. The scheme envisaged setting up of unit councils in those units which employ at least one hundred workers. The organisation where unit councils are set up include hotels, restaurants, hospitals, transport undertakings, (railways, air, sea, road transport services), educational institutions, ports and docks, provident fund and pension organisations, banks, insurance companies, municipalities, warehousing corporations etc.

The scheme provides for unit level councils. These councils are basically set up to eliminate factors which hinder progress and hamper operations. Efforts are made to improve methods of operations. Under this scheme of unit councils, each unit council consists of an equal number of representatives of management and workers. The actual number of the representatives is determined by the management in consultation with the recognised trade union, registered trade unions or the workers as per the needs. However, the total number of representatives does not exceed twelve. The management's representatives are nominated by the management who are from the concerned unit.

The decisions of a unit council are taken on the basis of consensus and not by the process of voting. The unsettled matters are referred to the joint council for consideration. Every decision of a unit council is implemented by the concerned parties within a period of a month, unless otherwise stated in the decision itself. The management makes necessary arrangements for the recording of minutes of the meetings and designate one of its representatives as a secretary for this purpose. The secretary is entrusted the responsibility to report on the action taken on the decisions at the subsequent meetings of the council.

A unit once formed, functions for a period of two years. The council can meet as frequently as is necessary but at least once in a month. The Chairman of the council is a nominee of the management while worker members of the council elect a vice-chairman from amongst themselves. The functions of the unit councils are more or less similar to those of joint councils. However, the main functions of a unit council are to create necessary conditions for attaining higher productivity and efficiency and to provide better customer services. Other functions performed by the unit councils are mentioned below :

(1) To create conditions for healthy employer-employee relations.

(2) To create and improve conditions for reducing absenteeism and recommend measures for the purpose.

(3) To identify areas of inadequate or inferior services and to take necessary constructive and corrective steps to eliminate the contributing factors and to evolve improved methods of operations.

(4) To institute a proper and suitable system of rewards for eliminating pilferage and all types of corruption.

(5) To ensure effective flow of adequate two-way communication between the management and workers for making the working of unit councils successful

(6) To suggest measures for improving the physical conditions of working such as lighting, ventilation, internal lay-out, setting up of customers' service points etc.

(7) To make recommendations for improving health, safety and welfare measures for the efficient working of the unit.

(h) Co-partnership : Under co-partnership, workers/employees are made equal partners i.e. owners of the organisation in which they work as employees. In co-partnership, workers or employees participate in the equity capital of their organisation. The shares are allotted to them either on cash payment basis or in-lieu of various incentives payable in cash. Thus, they become the shareholders of their organisation and can exercise control over it as other shareholders do.

The workers by becoming co-partners can participate in both i.e. sharing of profits and participating in management as shareholders. In this way, workers are given a higher status and they are connected with their organisation in a dual capacity. They, thus, can elect their representatives as directors and protect their interests. This helps to create better understanding between the management and employees which is essential for good industrial relations. It also helps in integrating the employees with their organisation and become the part-owner of the organisation to the extent of their shareholding. However, the workers do not get real control over the management and they cannot participate in management because of their negligible shareholding. The scope of workers' participation in management through co-partnership is quite limited.

(i) Auto-management : Under Auto-management scheme, workers are given wider powers in management. The industrial unit is established by the State but the day-to-day management is entrusted in the hands of workers working in the unit. Various targets e.g. production, sales etc. are decided at the government level, but other activities and functions are managed by the workers collectively. It is obvious that this method of workers' participation in management is suitable in socialist or communist countries. It exists in Yugoslavia, but it is not suitable to the Indian Economic System.

4.10 LEVELS OF WORKERS' PARTICIPATION IN MANAGEMENT

Workers' participation in management is important for maintaining smooth and healthy industrial relations. It helps workers to protect their interests, management and workers are benefited thereby. Workers' participation is possible at all levels of management. Much depends upon the nature of functions, the strength of the workers, the attitudes of the trade unions and also that of management. The areas and degrees of workers' participation can differ very considerably at different levels depending upon the circumstances, needs and so on.

Broadly speaking, there can be four stages of participation. At the initial stage, participation may be informative and associative participation. In such type of participation, the members are entitled to receive information, to give and discuss suggestions on the general economic condition of their organisation, the state of market production, sales programmes, organisation, long-term plans of growth and development etc.

At the consultative participation level, the workers are consulted on various matters such as welfare facilities, adoption of new technology and the problems emanating from it, safety measures etc. These aspects are directly related to the workers.

In administrative participation, there is a greater degree of sharing of authority and responsibility of management functions. In such participation, the members are given a little more autonomy in exercising administrative and supervisory powers in respect of certain matters like welfare and safety measures, operation of training and development programmes, preparation of schedules of working hours, breaks, holidays etc.

Decision-making participation is the highest form of participation. However, the management always likes to maintain its decision-making authority intact. The workers' participation in management involves participation through representatives of workers. Hence, its level can be considered in this context also. Generally, there can be three levels at which workers' participation in management can take place :

(a) **Shop-floor Level :** At shop-floor, shop-floor councils or committees are constituted. In such committees, the representatives of management and workers are included. They consider and discuss various matters, problems relating to a particular shop.

(b) **Plant Level :** There are many plants of an organisation or company which are located in different geographical areas. When this is the situation, plant level participation of workers in management proves to be useful and advantageous for maintaining good industrial relations. Where a company or an enterprise has a single plant, plant level participation is not needed. Various matters, problems are dealt at the plant level which have relevance for all shop-floors and they cannot be solved at the shop-floor level.

(c) **Enterprise Level :** At enterprise level, workers' participation is needed for constructive cooperation. Such participation can be in the forms of management committees, co-partnership or in the form of representation of workers at the level of Board of Directors.

4.11 BENEFITS OR ADVANTAGES AND ROLE OF WORKERS' PARTICIPATION IN MANAGEMENT

The basic idea or principle behind workers' participation in management is to increase the workers' influence in the management of an enterprise or an organisation to which they belong in order to solve their problems relating to their work. The following points make clear the benefits or advantages of workers' participation in management.

(a) It helps to promote good and healthy industrial relations for creating and maintaining industrial peace.

(b) It creates a better understanding in workers about their role, responsibilities and place in the process of attainment of organisational goals. It, in turn, leads to workers' commitment to their work and toward their organisation.

(c) It helps to improve the quality of decision making as workers/employees can offer useful suggestions and recommendations regarding the working of the organisation and for solving their problems.

(d) It eliminates the differences of opinion between workers and their management and facilitates team work.

(e) When workers' participation is effective, it increases a sense of confidence and trust in the minds of workers towards the management. As a result, workers give their full cooperation and accept change without much resistance. This also helps to avoid strikes and lockouts.

(f) When workers cooperate fully and whole heartedly, it leads to higher productivity and efficiency.

(g) Workers' participation in management satisfies the social and esteem needs of workers.

All the above mentioned advantages or benefits themselves make clear the role of workers' participation in management. Workers' participation in management is generally recognised as a measure to promote cooperation between management and workers to serve two basic purposes, one economic and the other moral and social. The former is to ensure increased production and productivity and the latter, increased recognition of the importance of the human element in the industrial field.

Besides these two purposes, better participation and greater responsibility in the decision making process and in the working of the organisation on the part of workers tend to develop in them organisational loyalty, confidence, trust and honesty, a favourable attitude towards their officers and also a sense of involvement in the organisation. This leads to industrial peace and helps to establish industrial democracy. Workers' participation in management serves as a means of self-realisation in work and it meets the psychological needs of workers. Workers' participation helps to establish appropriate two way communication between management and workers which is useful for solving their problems in the proper manner. For peaceful development and growth of organisations and also of the economy on a democratic basis, it is very essential that workers' participation in management should be accepted as a fundamental principle and an urgent need.

POINTS TO REMEMBER

1. **Pre-requisites for Successful Working of Workers' Participation in Management**

    (a) The attitude of an organisation/management should be constructive and progressive. It must sincerely and whole heartedly accept the concept of workers' participation and must be prepared to give a fair trial to the schemes of workers' participation.

    (b) Both parties should have genuine faith, mutual trust in the system and in each other. Moreover, they must be willing to work together.

    (c) There should be progressive management and it should recognise its obligations, responsibilities etc. towards their unions.

    (d) Trade union must be strong and democratic with a genuine and prudent leadership. The union leaders should have genuine desire to participate in the management. The attitude of union leaders should be positive, cooperative and not aggressive.

    (e) There should be closely and mutually formulated objectives for successful participation by management as well as trade unions.

    (f) There should be effective two-way communication for making the workers' participation successful. For that purpose, frequent meetings of representatives of workers and their employers/management should be held to discuss various issues relating to workers' participation schemes and to conduct negotiations for the solution of pending problems. Both the parties should make all the efforts to develop a favourable attitude towards the schemes of participative management.

(g) Workers should be given proper education and training as regards the schemes of workers participation. Along with workers, supervisory staff should also be associated with the management.

(h) The follow-up actions on the decisions of the participating forums should be ensured.

(i) There should be full recognition of the rights and claims of both the parties. Workers should no doubt be conscious of their rights, but at the same time, emphasis must also be laid on their responsibilities.

2. Objectives of Workers' Participation in Management

(a) To develop good industrial relations.

(b) To create and increase better understanding among the workers about their role and place in the process of attainment of organisational goals and objectives.

(c) To stimulate workers for higher productivity for the benefits of themselves for the advantage of their organisations and society at large.

(d) To satisfy the workers' social and esteem needs.

(e) To create among the workers the feeling of dignity and self-respect.

(f) To strengthen labour-management co-operation for maintaining industrial peace and harmony.

(g) To establish industrial democracy.

(h) To avoid external interference.

(i) To build dynamic human resources systematically.

(j) To share financial and other information about the organisation for the purpose of collective bargaining.

3. Forms or Methods of Workers' Participation in Management

(a) Works Committee

(b) Joint Management Councils

(c) Workers' Participation on the Board of Directors

(d) Suggestion Scheme

(e) Shop Councils

(f) Joint Councils

(g) Unit Councils

(h) Co-partnership

(i) Auto-management

4. **Levels of Workers' Participation in Management**

(a) Shop-floor Level

(b) Plant Level

(c) Enterprise Level

5. **Objectives of Workers Education**

(a) To assist workers to acquire skills, knowledge, attitudes etc. necessary for collective work performance.

(b) To enhance existing knowledge and performance capabilities of workers.

(c) To bring skills, capabilities of workers up to a standard for the present and future job assignments.

(d) To increase the efficiency, competency, and productivity of workers.

(e) To develop stronger and more effective trade unions through better well trained officials and more enlightened members for strengthening the bonds of loyalty to the trade unions.

(f) To equip the workers to take its place in democratic society and to fulfil its social and economic responsibilities.

(g) To promote among workers a greater and proper understanding of the problems of their economic environment and their privileges and obligations as the members of their trade unions.

QUESTIONS FOR DISCUSSION

Q.1 What do you mean by Workers' Education ? What is the rationale behind Workers' Education scheme in India ?

Q.2 State and explain the nature and objectives of Workers' Education.

Q.3 Explain fully Workers' Education Scheme in India. What are its objectives ?

Q.4 Explain the constitution and functions of the C.B.W.E.

Q.5 Explain the meaning and importance of workers' participation in management.

Q.6 Describe the pre-requisites for successful working of workers' participation in management.

Q.7 What is 'Workers' Participation in Management'? Explain its objectives.

Q.8 Explain the forms or methods of workers' participation in management.

Q.9 Explain various levels of workers' participation in management.

Q.10 Discuss the benefits and role of workers' participation in management.

Q.11 Write short notes on the following :

  (a) Meaning and objectives of Workers' Education.

  (b) Nature of Workers' Education Scheme in India.

  (c) Constitution and functions of the CBWE.

  (d) Concept of workers' participation in management.

  (e) Pre-requisites of workers' participation in management.

  (f) Forms and levels of workers' participation in management.

  (g) Benefits of workers' participation in management.

  (h) Role of workers' participation in labour welfare.

QUESTIONS FROM PREVIOUS EXAMINATIONS

Q.1 Describe the welfare, safety and health provisions under the Plantation Labour Act, 1951 and Mines Act, 1952.   **[Dec-2012]**

Q.2 Define the term 'Workers' Participation in Management'. Explain the role of WPM in the Industrial Organisation.   **[April-2013]**

Q.3 Write short notes on (any three) :   **[April-2013]**

  (a) Corporate Social Responsibility

  (b) Ethics and Welfare

  (c) Health provisions under the Mines Act, 1952

  (d)   Concept of Industrial Hygiene

  (e) Mental Health

Q.4 Explain the Meaning of the term Workers Participation in Management with its Aims and Objectives.   **[April-2006]**

Q.5 Explain the term WPM. How can Labour Welfare be achieved through WPM?
                                                                                [Dec-2007]

Q.6 Write Short Notes on Workers Education Scheme.   **[April-2007]**

Q.7 Explain the Concept of Workers Participation in Management. How far this has been successful in our Country? Explain with examples.   **[April-2010, 2011]**

Q.8 Write Short Notes on the Concept of Workers Education.   **[April-2011]**

✍ ✍ ✍

Chapter **5**...

Labour Welfare Funds and The Maharashtra Labour Welfare Fund Act, 1953

Contents ...

Learning Objectives

At the end of the chapter, you will understand:
- Provisions of the Maharashtra Labour Welfare Fund Act of 1953
- Constitution and Administration of the Maharashtra Workers Welfare Board
- Meaning and Constitution of Labour Welfare Fund
- Powers of Welfare Commissioner
- Meaning, objectives and importance of Social Security
- Social Security Provisions in India

5.1 Introduction

Labour welfare is one of the major aspects of national programmes towards bettering the life of working class and creating a comfortable work environment for them. Various welfare measures and activities are undertaken by the state government and association of workers for increasing the standard of living and for the improvement of their economic and social well-being. These measures of workers activities are known as 'Welfare Work'.

Welfare work includes the measures introduced for improving the health, safety, general well-being and efficiency of labour beyond the expected minimum standards laid down by labour legislation. It includes services, facilities and amenities which may be established in or in the vicinity of undertakings or work places to enable the person employed in them to perform their work in healthy, congenial (i.e. sympathetic and suitable) surroundings and provided them with various amenities conducive to good health, mental peace and high morale. To meet these purposes various labour welfare measures have been introduced. Such measures can be classified into the following two categories:

(a)   Statutory labour welfare measures.

(b)   Voluntary or non-statutory labour welfare measures.

Statutory labour welfare measures include different legislations. Employers are statutorily required to comply with provisions of various labour welfare amenities under different labour laws e.g. The Factories Act - 1948, the Plantation and Labour Act – 1951, Mines Act – 1952, etc. The Maharashtra Labour Welfare Fund of 1953 is one such labour law which provides for the constitution of a fund for financing of various activities to promote welfare of labour in Maharashtra state. In this chapter we will study and discuss the various provisions of this Act and certain aspects related to social security.

5.2 PROVISIONS OF THE MAHARASHTRA LABOUR WELFARE FUND ACT OF 1953

The Central Government has set up statutory labour welfare funds for certain industries, e.g. coal mines, mica mines, cine workers, bide workers under different Acts. The Coal Mines Provident Fund and Bonus Act of 1948, the Iron Ore Mines, Manganese Ore Mines and Chrome Ore Mines Labour Welfare Fund Act of 1976, the Limestone and Dolomite Mines Labour Fund Act of 1972, the Beedi Workers Welfare Fund Act of 1976 are some of the Central Government's Acts under which labour Welfare Funds have been constituted.

Statutory labour welfare funds have also been constituted by some of the state Governments by passing certain Acts. In Maharashtra, the Bombay Labour Welfare Fund Act was passed in 1953 in order to provide for the constitution of a labour welfare fund for the financing of the activities to promote welfare of labour. This Act is now called as the Maharashtra Labour Welfare Fund Act, 1953.

5.2.1 Basic Objective of the M.L.W.F. Act of 1956

The basic objective of the Act is stated in the preamble of the Act which is as follows:

"An Act to provide for the constitution of a fund for the financing of activities to promote welfare of labour in the State of Maharashtra for conducting such activities and for certain other purposes."

5.2.2 Definitions of the Words, Terms, etc. as given in Section 2 of the Act

In Section 2 of the Act, the definitions of certain words, terms, etc. are given. These definitions are as follows:

(1) **"Board"** means the Maharashtra Labour Welfare Board constituted under Section 4; [Section 2 (1)].

(2) **"Contribution"** means the sum of money payable to the Board in accordance with the provisions of Section 6BB; {Section 2 (1 – A)}.

(3) **"Employee"** means any person who is employed for hire or reward to co any work, skilled or unskilled, manual, clerical, supervisory or technical in an establshment directly by the employer or through contractor or any other agency, but does not include any person,

(i) Who is employed mainly in a managerial capacity,

(ii) Who, being employed in a supervisory capacity, draws wages exceeding three thousand five hundred rupees per mensem or exercises powers or carries out, either by the nature of the duties attached to the office, or by reason of the powers vested in him, functions mainly of a managerial nature, or

(iii) Who is employed as an apprentice under the Apprentices Act, 196 [Section 2 (2)].

(4) **"Employer"** means any person who employs either directly or through another person either on behalf of himself or any other person, one or more emplcyees in an establishment and includes,

(i) In a factory, any person named under Section 7(i) (f) of the Factories Act, 1948, (LXIII of 1948), as the manager.

(ii) In any establishment, any person responsible to the owner for the supervision and control of the employees or for the payment of wages: [Section 2 (3)].

(5) **"Establishment"** means-

(i) A factory;

(ii) A tramway or 'motor omnibus service or a motor transport undertaking tc which the Motor Transport Workers Act, 1961, applies: and

(iii) Any establishment within the meaning of the Maharashtra Shops and Establishments Act, 1943, (Mah. LXXIX of 1948), which employs, or on any working day during the preceding twelve months, employed five or more persons including the establishments which have been granted exemption partly or wholly under the provisio to Section 4 of that Act [Section 2 (4)]

It is provided that, any such establishment shall continue to be an establishment for the purpose of this Act, not withstanding a reduction in the number of persons to less than five at any subsequent time [Provisio 1 to Section 2 (4)].

It is also provided further that, where for a continuous period of not less than three months the number or persons employed therein has been less than five such establishment shall cease to be an establishment for the purpose of this Act with effect from the beginning of the month following the expiry of the said period of three months, but the employer shall within one month from the date of such cessation, intimate by registered post the fact thereof to such authority as the State Government may specify in this behalf [Provisio 2 to Section 2 (4)].

For the removal of doubt, it is hereby declared that where an establishment has different branches or departments, all such branches or departments whether situated in the same premises or different premises shall be treated as parts of the same establishment [Explanation to Section 2 (4)].

(6) **"Factory"** as defined in Section 2(m) of the Factories Act, 1948 (LXIII of 1948), includes any place wherein five or more persons are employed or working, and

(i) Wherein any manufacturing process is being carried on with the aid of power or is ordinarily so carried on;

(ii) Which is deemed to be a factory under Section 85 of the said Act [Section 2 (5)].

(7) **"Fund"** means Labour Welfare Fund constituted under Section 3; [Section 2 (6)]

(8) **"Independent member"** means a member of the Board who is not connected with the management of any establishment or who is not an employee, and includes an officer of Government nominated as a member; [Section 2 (7)].

(9) **"Inspector"** means an Inspector appointed under Section 12; [Section 2(8)].

(10) **"Unpaid accumulation"** means all payments due to the employees but not made to them within a period of three years from the date on which they became due whether before or after the commencement of this Act including the wages, and gratuity legally payable [but not including the amount of contribution if any, paid by an employer to a provident fund established under the Employees Provident Funds Act, 1952 [Section 2 (10)].

(11) **"Wages"** as defined in Section 2 (vi) of the Payment of Wages Act 1936; (4 of 1936), and includes bonus payable under the Payment of Bonus Act, 1965 (21 of 1965) [Section 2(11)].

(12) **"Welfare Commissioner"** means the Welfare Commissioner appointed under Section 11 [Section 2 (12)].

5.2.3 Application and Scope of the Act

This Act has been passed to provide for the constitution of a fund for financing the activities to promote welfare of the labour/ workers in the State of Maharashtra.

The Act applies to factories covered under Section 2 (m) of the Factories Act of 1948, establishments within the meaning of the Bombay Shops and Establishments Act of 1948, and motor transport undertakings under the Motor Transport Workers Act of 1961, which employs on any working day during the preceding twelve months five or more persons. However, if the number of persons employed becomes less than five for a continuous period of not less than three months then such establishment is not covered under the provision of this Act.

Person employed in any skilled, unskilled, manual, clerical and technical work are covered under this Act. It may be noted that the persons employed in a managerial or administrative function or engaged in a supervisory capacity drawing more then Rs. Three Thousand and Five Hundred per month and also an apprentice under the Apprentices Act of 1961 are excluded from the purview of this Act.

This Act is considered as an important milestone for labour welfare. Under this Act, the government is required to constitute the Labour Welfare Fund. The Fund consists of:

(a) All fines realised from the employees

(b) Unpaid accumulations

(c) Six monthly tripartite contributions payable as on 30th June and 31st December

(d) Voluntary donations, if any

(e) Any sum borrowed under Section 8 of the Act

(f) Any loan, grant-in-aid or subsidy paid by the Government of Maharashtra

In the following table, various aspects of the Labour Welfare Fund are given section wise from which we come to know the scope, application, extent, etc of the Act and the topics in respect of which provisions have been made in this Act.

Table 5.1 : The Maharashtra Labour Welfare Fund Act, 1953

Section	Particulars
1.	Short title, extent and commencement.
2.	Definitions.
3.	Welfare Fund.
4.	Board.
5.	Disqualifications and removal.
6.	Resignation of office of member and filling up of casual vacancies.
6-AA.	Power to appoint committees.
6-A.	Unpaid accumulations and claims thereof.
6-BB.	Contributions.
6-B.	Interest on unpaid accumulations or fines after notice of demand.
7.	Vesting and application of fund.
8.	Power of Board to borrow.
9.	Investment of Fund.
10.	Directions by State Government to Board.
11.	Appointment and Powers of Welfare Commissioner.
12.	Appointment of Inspectors.
13.	Absorption of the existing staff under Commissioner of Labour.
14.	Appointment of clerical and other staff by Board.
15.	Power of State Government to remove any person on staff of Board.
16.	Power of State Government to authorised officers to call for records, etc.
17.	Mode of recovery of sums payable to Board, etc.
17 A.	Penalty for obstructing inspection in discharge or Inspector's duties or for failure to produce documents, etc.
17-B.	Provisions relating to jurisdiction.
18.	Supersession of Board.
19.	Rules.
20.	Members of Board, Welfare Commissioner, Inspectors and all officers and servants of Board to be public servants.
21.	Protection to persons acting in good faith.
22.	Exemptions.
23.	Amendment of Section 8 of Act IV of 1936.

5.2.4 Provisions of the Act Relating to Welfare Fund

Provision have been made in the Act relating to Welfare Fund in different sections, e.g. Section 3 [Meaning, Constitution of Welfare Fund, Section 6 B-B [Contribution], Section 7 [Vesting and application of Fund] etc. These provisions are given below.

5.2.4.1 Constitution of Welfare Fund [Section 3]

(1) The State Government shall constitute a fund called the Labour Welfare Fund, and notwithstanding anything contained in any other law for the time being in force or in any contract or instrument, all unpaid, accumulations shall be paid [at such intervals as may be prescribed to the Board, which shall keep a separate account therefore until claims thereto have been decided in the manner provided in Section 6A, and the other sums specified in sub-section (2) shall be paid into the Fund.

(2) The Fund shall consist of :

(a) All fines realised from the employees;

(b) Unpaid accumulations transferred to the Fund under Section 6A;

(c) Any penal interest paid under Section 6B;

(d) Any contribution paid under Section 6 BB;

(e) Any voluntary donations;

(f) Any fund transferred under Section (5) of Section 7;

(g) Any sum borrowed under Section 8;

(h) Any loan, grant-in-aid or subsidy paid by the State Government [Section 3(2)]. The sums specified in sub-section (2) shall be paid or collected by such agencies, at such intervals and in such manner and the account of the Fund shall be maintained and audited in such manner as may be prescribed [Section 3 (3)].

5.2.4.2 Unpaid Accumulations and Claims thereto [Section 6–A]

The Welfare Fund consists of the fines realised from the employees, contributions by the employers and employees as per the provisions of the Act, voluntary donations etc. Besides these amounts, it consists of unpaid accumulations. The provisions relating to unpaid accumulations and claims thereto have been made in Section-6 A of the Act. These provisions are as under.

(1) All unpaid accumulations shall be deemed to be abandoned property.

(2) Any unpaid accumulations paid to the Board in accordance with the Provisions of section 3 shall on such payment, discharge an employer of the liability to make payment to an employee in respect thereof, but to the extent only of the amount paid to the Board, and the liability to make payment to the employee to the extent aforesaid shall subject to the succeeding provisions of this section be deemed to be transferred to the Board.

(3) As soon as possible after the payment of any unpaid accumulation is made to the Board, the Board shall by notice (containing such particulars as may be prescribed):

(a) Exhibited on the notice-board of the factory or establishment in which the unpaid accumulations were earned, and

(b) Also published in any two newspapers circulating and in the language commonly understood in the area in which the factory or establishment in which the unpaid accumulation was earned is situated, or in such other manner as may be prescribed, regard being had to the amount of the claim.

Invite claims by employees for any payment due to them. The notice shall be inserted in the manner aforesaid in June and December of every year, for a period of three years from the date of the payment of the unpaid accumulation to the Board.

(4) If any question arises whether the notice referred to in sub-section (3) given as required by that sub-section, a certificate of the Board that it was so given shall be conclusive.

(5) If a claim is received whether in answer to the notices or otherwise, within a period of four years from the date of first publication of the notice in respect of such claim, the Board shall transfer such claim to the Authority appointed under Section 15 of the Payment of Wages Act, 1936 (IV of 1936) having jurisdiction in the area in which the factory or establishment situated an Authority shall proceed to adjudicate upon, and decide, such claim. In hearing such claim, the Authority shall have the power, conferred by, and follow the procedure (in so far as it is applicable) followed in giving effect to the provisions of that Act.

(6) If the Authority aforesaid is satisfied that any such claim is valid so that the right to receive payment is established, it shall decide that the unpaid accumulation in relation to which the claim is made shall cease to be deemed to be abandoned property and shall order the Board to pay the whole of the dues claimed, or such part there of as the Authority decides are properly due, to the employee; and the Board shall make payment accordingly.

Provided that, the Board shall not be liable to pay any sum in excess of that paid under sub-section (1) of Section 3 to the Board, as unpaid accumulations, in respect of the claim.

(7) If a claim for payment is refused, the employee shall have a right of appeal in Greater Mumbai to the Court of Small Causes, and elsewhere to the District Court, and the Board shall comply with any order made in appeal. An appeal shall lie within sixty days of the decision of the Authority.

(8) The decision of the Authority, subject to appeal aforesaid, and the decision in appeal of the Court of Small Causes, or as the case may be, the District Court, shall be final and conclusive as to the right to receive payment the liability of the Board to pay and also as to the amount, if any.

(9) If no claim is made within the time specified sub-section (5), or a claim has been duly refused as aforesaid by the Authority, or on appeal by the Court, then the unpaid accumulations in respect of such claim shall accrue to, and vest in, the State as bona vacantia, and shall thereafter, without further assurance be deemed to be transferred to, form part of the Fund.

5.2.4.3 *Contributions Payable by an Employee and an Employer under this Act [Section 6–BB]*

Provisions relating to contributions payable towards the Welfare Fund have been made in Section 6 – BB of the Act. The rates of contributions are revised from time to time according to the needs and circumstances by amending the Act. The rates have been revised in 2003 by amending the Act.

The revised rates of contributions and other details are gives in the following box for your information.

MAHARASHTRA LABOUR WELFARE BOARD

OFFICE OF THE WELFARE COMMISSIONER

Hutatma Babu Genu Kamgar Kreeda -Bhavan, Senapati Bapat Marg, Elphinstone,

Mumbai 400 013. Tel. Nos. 24306717/24227758/24360738 Fax No. 24210019.

The employers of Factories, Shops, Commercial Establishments, Hotels, Restaurants, Banks, Hospitals, Boards, Corporations and all the other establishments which are coming within the purview of the Bombay Labour Welfare Fund Act, 1953 are hereby informed the said Act is recently Amended in 2003 vide Mah. Act No. XXIV of 2003. As per the said Amendment the rates of Employees' and Employers' Contribution have been increased from 31st December, 2000. The revised (enhanced) rates are as under:

Particulars	Employees' Contribution	Employers' Contribution	Total
Employees drawing wages upto and inclusive of ₹ 3000/- P.m.	6.00	18.00	24.00
Employees drawing wages above ₹ 3,000/- p.m.	12.00	3.00	48.00

The employers are further informed that the contribution may be paid at enhanced rate from 31st December, 2000. If they have paid the same at old rate, the difference between old rate and revised rate may be paid immediately by Cheque /DD at the above address between 10.30 a.m. to 5.30 p.m. and cash will be accepted between 10.30 a.m to 3-00 p.m.

Note : Cheque / DD should be drawn in favour of

"MAHARASHTRA LABOUR WELFARE FUND " only.

Sd/-

(Ankush More)

Welfare Commissioner

Provisions of Section 6-BB relating to contributions are given below :

(1) The contribution payable under this Act in respect of an employee in an establishment shall comprise contribution, payable by the employer (hereinafter referred to as 'the employer's contribution') contribution payable by such employee (hereinafter referred to as "the employee's contribution") and the contribution payable by the State Government, and shall be paid to the Board and form part of the Fund [Section 6 B-B(1)].

(2) The amount of contribution payable every six months in respect of every employee and an employer for each such employee shall be at the following rates, namely-

(a) (i) In respect of employee drawing wages upto and inclusive of three thousand rupees per mensem, six rupees, and

(ii) In respect of an employee drawing wages exceeding three thousand rupees per mensem, twelve rupees.

Only if the name of such employee stands on the register of an establishment on the 30th June and 31st December respectively; [Section 6 B-B 2 (a)]

It is provided that the State Government may, on receipt of a proposal from the Board, by notification in the official Gazette, increase once in every three years the rate of employee's contribution so, however, that, such increase shall not exceed 30 per cent of the rates of contribution [Proviso to section 6 B-B 2 (a)].

(b) In respect of an employer for each employee referred to in sub-clauses (i) and (ii) of clause (a) thrice the amount of contribution payable by an employee; [Section 6 B-B 2 (b)].

(3) Every employer shall pay to the Board both the employer's contribution and the employee's contribution in accordance with the provisions of sub-section (2) before the 15th day of July and 15th day of January, as the case may be [Section 6 B-B(3)].

(4) Notwithstanding anything contained in any other enactment but subject to the provisions of this Act and any rules, the employer shall in the case of any such deduction shall be deemed to be a deduction authorized by or under the payment of Wages Act, 1936 { Section 6 B-B (4)].

It is provided that, no such deduction shall be made in excess of the amount of the contribution payable by such employee, nor shall it be made from any wages other than the wages for the months of June and December [Proviso 1 to section 6 B-B (4)].

It is provided further that, if through inadvertence or otherwise, no deduction has been made from the wages of an employee for the months aforesaid, such deduction may be made from the wages of such employee for any subsequent month or months with the permission in writing of the inspector appointed under this Act [Proviso 2 to section 6 B-B (4)].

(5) Notwithstanding any contract to the contrary, no employer shall deduct the employer's contribution from any wages payable to an employee or otherwise recover it from the employee [Section 6 B-B (5)].

(6) Any sum duly deducted by an employer from the wages of an employee under this section shall be deemed to have been entrusted to him by the employee for the purpose of paying the contribution is respect of which it was deducted [Section 6 B-B (6)].

(7) An employer shall pay the employee's and the employee's contribution to the Board by cheque, money-order or in cash, and he shall bear the expenses of remitting to the Board such contributions [Section 6 B-B (7)].

(8) The Welfare Commissioner shall submit to the State Government as soon as possible after the end of July and January every year in the prescribed form a statement showing the total amount of the employer's contribution and the employee's contribution in respect of employees in each establishment. On receipt of the statement from the Welfare Commissioner, the State Government shall pay to the Board a contribution of an amount equal to half the employee's contribution for the period from the 31st December 2000 to the 31st March 2003; and an amount equal to twice the employee's contribution with effect from the 1st April 2003, in respect of every employee referred to in sub-clauses (i) and (ii) of clause (a) of sub-section (2); [Section 6 B-B (8)]

5.2.4.4 *Interest on Unpaid Accumulations or Fines after Notice of Demand [Section 6 (B)]*

(1) If an employer does not pay to the Board any amount of unpaid accumulations, or fines realised from the employee or the amount of the employer's and employee's contribution under Section 6 BB within the time he is required by or under the provisions of this Act to pay it, the Welfare Commissioner may cause to be served a notice on such employer to pay the amount within the period specified therein, which shall not be less than thirty days from the date of service of such notice [Section 6 B (1)].

(2) If the employer fails, without sufficient cause to pay any such amount within the period specified in the notice, he shall, in addition to that amount, pay to the Board simple interest.

(a) In the case of a failure to pay any amount of unpaid accumulations of fines realised from the employees,

(i) For the first three months, at one and a half per cent of the said amount for each completed month, after the last date by which he should have paid it according to the notice; and.

(ii) Thereafter, at two per cent of that amount for each completed month, during the time he continues to make default in the payment of that amount.

(b) In the case of a failure to pay any amount of the employer's and employee's contributions under Section 6 BB –

(i) For the first three months, at one and a half per cent of the said amount for each completed month, after the last date by which he should have paid it in accordance with the provisions of sub-section (3) of section 6 BB; and

(ii) Thereafter, at two per cent of that amount for each complete month, during the time he continues to make default in the payment of that amount [Section 6 B (2)].

It is provided that, the Welfare Commissioner may, subject to such conditions as may be prescribed, remit the whole or any part of the penalty in respect of any period [Proviso to Section 6 B (2)].

5.2.4.5 *Vesting and Utilisation or Application of 'Welfare Fund' [Section 7]*

Provision of Section 7 (2) makes clear the measures on which the expenditure can be incurred out of the Labour Welfare Fund constituted under this Act. The provisions of Section 7 also make clear the vesting of the Fund. The provisions of Section 7 are as follows:

(1) The fund shall vest in and be held and applied by the Board of Trustees subjects to the provisions and for the purpose of this Act. The moneys therein shall be utilised by the Board to defray the cost of carrying out measures which may be specified by the State Government from time to time to promote the welfare of labour and of their dependents [Section 7 (1)].

(2) Without prejudice to the generality of sub-section (1) the moneys in the Fund may be utilised by the Board to defray expenditure on the following:

(a) Community and social education centers including reading rooms and libraries;

(b) Community necessities;

(c) Games and sport;

(d) Excursions, tours and holiday homes;

(e) Entertainment and other forms of recreations;

(f) Home industries and subsidiary occupations for women and unemployed persons.

(g) Corporate activities of a social nature.

(h) Cost of administering the Act including the salaries, allowances, pension, provident fund and gratuity and other fringe benefits of the staff appointed for the purpose of the Act; and

(f) Such other objects as would in the opinion of the State Government improve the standard of living and ameliorate the social conditions of labour [Section 7 (2)].

It is provided that the Fund shall not be utilised in financing any measure which the employer is required under any law for the time being in force to carry out [Proviso 1 to Section 7 (2)].

It is provided further that unpaid accumulations and fines shall be paid to the Board and be expended by it under this Act notwithstanding anything contained in the payment of Wages Act, 1936 (IV of 1936), or any other low for the time being in force [Section 2 to Section 7 (2)].

(3) The Board may, with the approval of the State Government, make a grant of the Fund to any employer local authority or any other body in aid of any activity for the welfare of labour approved by the State Government [Section 7 (3)].

(4) If any question arises whether any particular expenditure is or is not dubitable to the Fund, the matter shall be referred to the State Government and the decision given by the State Government shall be final [Section 7 (4)].

(5) It shall be lawful for the Board to continue any activity financed from the labour welfare fund of any establishment, if the said fund is duly transferred to the Board [Section 7 (5)].

5.2.4.6 *Power of Board to Borrow [Section 8]*

The Board may from, time to time with the, previous sanction of the State Government and subject to the provisions of this Act and to such conditions as may be specified in this behalf borrow any sum required for the purpose of this Act. "

5.2.4.7 *Investment of Fund [Section 9]*

Where the Fund or any portion thereof cannot be applied at any early date for fulfilling the objects of the Act, the Board shall invest the same in any of the securities specified in clauses (a) to (d) and (f) of section 20 of the Indian Trusts Act, 1882 (II of 1882)".

5.2.4.8 Directions by State Government to Board [Section 10]

The State Government may give the Board such directions as in its option are necessary or expedient in connection with expenditure from the Fund or for carrying out the other purposes of the Act. It shall be duty of the Board to comply with such directions.'

5.2.4.9 Amendment of Section 8 of the Payment of Wages Act of 1936 [Section 23]

Section 8 of the payment of wages Act of 1936 pertains to deductions on account of the fines. Section 23 of the M.L.W.F. Act of 1953 makes it clear that all fines and realisations collected under the payment of wages Act of 1936 under section 8 (8) are required to be paid into the welfare fund. Of course, it is applicable to a factory or an establishment to which the M.L.W.F. Act of 1953 is applied. The exact provision of Section 23 of the M.L.W. F. Act of 1953 are as follows.

In Section 8 of the payment of Wages Act, 1936 (IV of 1936), to sub-section (8) the following shall be added, before the explanation, namely-

"but in the case of any factory or establishment to which the Maharashtra Labour Welfare Fund Act, 1953 (Mah XL of 1953), applied all such realisations shall be paid into the Fund constituted under the said Act".

5.3 PROVISIONS OF THE M.L.W.F. ACT OF 1953 RELATING TO "MAHARASHTRA LABOUR WELFARE BOARD"

The Maharashtra Labour Welfare Board (M.L.W. Board) is the corporate body constituted under this Act. This Board is responsible for conducting various welfare activities according to the provisions of this Act. The Board consists of not more than Twenty six members [Section 4 (1)].

The Welfare commissioner is appointed by the M.L.W Board with the previous approval of the State Government. He is the principle executive officer of the M.L.W. Board. The M.L.W. Board has to utilise the Fund for the measures, welfare activities mentioned in Section 7 of this Act.

Various provisions relating to the M.L.W. Board, its constitution, disqualifications and removal of a member, appointment and power of welfare commissioner, appointment of inspectors etc have been made in this Act. These provisions are given below for your information.

5.3.1 Provisions of Section 4 of the M.L.W.F Act of 1953 relating to Constitution of the M.L.W Board

Section 4 of this Act makes clear the constitution of the M.L.W. Board. This Board is constituted for the whole state of Maharashtra. The provisions of Section 4 are as follows:

(1) The State Government shall, by notification in the Official Gazette constitute the Board for the whole of the State of Maharashtra for the purpose of administering the Fund, and to carry on such other functions assigned to the Board by or under this Act. The Board shall consist of the following members, not exceeding twenty six in number namely :

   (a) Such number as may be prescribed of representative of employers and employees to be nominated by the State Government, provided that both employers and employers shall have equal representation on the Board.

   (b) Such number of independent members as may be prescribed, nominated by the State Government.

   (c) Such number of independent members as may be prescribed, nominated by the State Government to represent women.

   (d) The Principal Secretary or Secretary (Finance) or his nominee shall be the ex-officio member.

   (e) The Principal Secretary or Secretary (Labour) or his nominee shall be the ex-officio member [Section 4 (1)].

(2) The members of the Board shall elect one of its independent members as the Chairman of the Board [Section 4 (2)].

(3) Save as otherwise expressly provided by this Act, the term of office of the members of the Board shall be three years commencing on the date on, which the names are notified in the Official Gazette [Section 4 (3)].

(4) The allowances, if any, payable to the members of the Board shall be such as may be prescribed [Section 4 (4)].

(5) The Board shall be a body corporate by the name of the Maharashtra Labour Welfare Board having perpetual succession and a common seal, with power to acquire property both movable and immovable, and shall by the said name sue and be sued [Section 4 (5)].

(6) Notwithstanding anything contained in this section, until the Board for State of Maharashtra is duly constituted in accordance with the provision of sub-section (1),

the existing Board functioning and operating immediately before the commencement of the Maharashtra Labour Welfare Fund (Extension and Amendment) A 1961 (Mah. XXXVI of 1961), in any area of the State shall continue to function and operate in that area and shall be the Board for the purpose of this Act for that area; and on the constitution of the Board for the whole of State of Maharashtra under sub-section (1)-

(a) Such existing Board shall stand dissolved, and the members thereof shall vacate office.

(b) All properties, funds and dues which are vested or realisable by the Board so constituted;

(c) All rights and liabilities which were enforceable by or against the existing Board, shall be enforceable by or against the Board so constituted, and wherein any proceedings in any Court or Tribunal the existing Board is a party thereto, the Board so constituted shall be deemed to be substituted as a party to those proceedings, and

(d) The Welfare Commissioner and the other officers and servants of the existing Boards shall continue to be the Welfare Commissioner and officers and servants of the Board so constituted', but the terms and conditions of service of the "Welfare Commissioner and other officers and servants shall not, until duly altered by a competent authority, be less favourable under the Board so constituted than those admissible to them while in the service of the existing Board [Section 4 (6)].

Section 4 (5) makes it clear that the M.L.W. Board is a body corporate and it has perpetual succession and a common seal. This Board is empowered under this section to acquire property.

5.3.2 Provisions of Section 5 of the M.L.W.F Act of 1953 relating to Disqualification and Removal or a Member of the Board

(1) No person shall be chosen as, or continue to be a member of the Board who

(a) is a salaried official of the Board, or

(b) is or at any time has been adjudged insolvent or has suspended payment of his debts or has compounded with his creditors; or

(c) is found to be a lunatic or becomes of unsound mind; or

(d) is or has been convicted of any offence involving moral turpitude.

(2) The State Government may remove from office any member who :

    (a) is or has become subject to any of the disqualifications mentioned in sub-section (1), or

    (b) is absent without leave of the Board for more than three consecutive meetings of the Board [Section 5 (2)].

5.3.3 Resignation of Office by Member and Filling up of Casual Vacancies [Section 6]

(1) A member may resign his office by giving notice thereof in writing to the State Government and on such resignation being accepted shall be deemed to have vacated his office [Section 6 (1)].

(2) A casual vacancy in the office of a member shall be filled up, as soon as conveniently may be, by the authority concerned and a member so nominated shall hold office for the unexpired portion of, the term of the office of his predecessor [Section 6 (2)].

(3) No act or proceedings of the Board shall be questioned on the ground merely of the existence of any vacancy in, or any defect in constitution of the Board [Section 6 (3)].

5.3.4 Power to Appoint Committees

For the purpose of advising the Board in the discharge of its functions and also for carrying into effect any of the matters specified in, sub-section (2) of Section 7, the Board may constitute one or more Committees, of which at least one on each Committee shall be a member of the Board [Section 6 –A - A].

5.3.5 Appointment and Powers of Welfare Commissioner [Section 11]

    (i) The Welfare Commissioner shall be appointed by the Board with the previous approval of the State Government;

    (ii) The Welfare Commissioner shall be the principal executive officer of the Board;

    (iii) It shall be the duty of the Welfare Commissioner to ensure that the provisions of this Act and the rules made thereunder are duly carried out and for this purpose he shall have the power to issue such orders not inconsistent with the provision of the Act and Rules made thereunder as he deems fit including any order implementing the decisions taken by the Board under Act or Rules made thereunder.

5.3.6 Appointment of Inspectors and Powers of the Inspectors thus appointed under Section 12 of the M.L.W. Fund Act of 1953

(1) The State Government may appoint Inspectors to inspect records in connection with the sums payable into the Fund. Inspectors appointed, whether by a local authority or the State Government under the Maharashtra Shops and Establishments Act, 1948, (Mah.LXXIX of 1948), in relation to any area, shall be deemed to be also inspectors for the purposes of this Act, in respect of establishments to which this Act applies, and the local limits within which such Inspector shall exercise his functions under this Act shall be the area for which he is appointed under the said Act [Section 12 (1)].

(2) Any Inspector may-

(a) with such assistance, if any, as he thinks fit, enter at any reasonable t me any premises for carrying out the purposes of this Act;

(b) exercise such other powers as may be prescribed [Section 12 (2)].

5.3.7 Provisions of Section 13 relating to the Absorption of the Existing Staff under Commissioner of Labour

(1) The Board shall take over and employ such of the existing staff under the control of the Commissioner of Labour, Mumbai, as the State Government may direct and every person so taken, over and employed shall be subject to the provisions of this Act and the rules made thereunder;

Provided that:

(a) during the period of such employment all matters relating to pay, leave, retirement, allowances, pensions, provident fund and other conditions of service of the said staff shall be regulated by the Maharashtra Civil Services Rules or such, other rules as may be from time to time be made by the State Government.

(b) every such member shall have a right of appeal to the State Government against any order of reduction, dismissal or removal from service, fine or any other punishment [Section 13 (1)].

It is provided further that person so taken over may elect within the prescribed period that he desires to be governed by the rules made under this Act in respect of conditions of service of the staff appointed by the Board under this Act and on his electing to do so the provisions of the first proviso shall cease to apply to him [Proviso to Section 13 (1)].

(2) On the commencement of this Act in any area to which it is extended by the Maharashtra Labour Welfare Fund (Extension and Amendment) Act 1961, (Mah.XXXVI of 1961), the Board shall take over and employ such of the existing staff under the control of the Commissioner of Labour, Mumbai, as the State Government may direct, and every such person, so taken over and employed shall be subject to the like terms and conditions and to the same provisions as its sub-section (1), and to the other provisions of, this Act and the rules made thereunder [Section 13 (2)].

5.3.8 Appointment of Clerical and Other Staff by Board under Section 14

(1) The Board shall have power to appoint the necessary clerical and executive staff to carry out and supervise the activities financed from the Fund [Section 14 (1)].

It is provided that the expenses of the staff thus appointed and other administrative expenses shall not exceed a prescribed percentage of the annual income of the fund [Proviso to Section 14 (1)].

(2) The Board shall, with the approval of the State Government, make regulations regarding the method of recruitment, pay and allowances, and other conditions of service of the members of its staff (other than the Welfare Commissioner and the inspectors) [Section 14 (2)].

It is provided that, until the regulations are so made, the conditions of service of such staff shall be governed by rules made by the State Government in this behalf [Proviso to Section 14 (2)].

5.3.9 Power of State Government to Remove Any Person on Staff of Board under Section 15

" The State Government shall have the power to remove any person whom it may deem unsuitable from the service of the Board and to make an appointment in respect of whom more than one-third of the members of the Board have not agreed."

5.3.10 Power of State Government or Authorised Officer to Call for Records etc. under Section 16

" The State Government or any officer authorised by the State Government may call for the records of the Board, inspect the same and may supervise the working of the Board."

5.3.11 Mode of Recovery of Sums Payable to Board etc. under Section 17

Any sum payable [to the Board] or into the Fund under this Act shall, without prejudice to any other mode of recovery, be recoverable on behalf of the Board as an arrear of the revenue.

5.3.12 Penalty for Obstructing Inspection in Discharge of Inspector's Duties or for Failure to Produce Document, etc. under Section 17-A

Any person who willfully obstructs an inspector in the exercise of his powers or discharge of his duties under this Act or fails to produce for inspection on demand by an inspector any registers, records or other documents maintained in pursuance of the provisions of this Act or the rules made thereunder or to supply to him on demand true copies of any such documents shall, on conviction, be punished:

(a) for the first offence, with imprisonment for a term which may extend to three months, or with fine which may extend to five hundred rupees, or with both; and

(b) for a second or subsequent offences, with imprisonment for a term which may extend to six months, or with fine which may extend to one thousand rupees, or with both [Section 17 –A].

It is provided that, in the absence of special and adequate reasons to the contrary to be mentioned in the judgment of the Court, in any case where the offender is sentenced to a fine only, the amount of fine shall not be less than fifty rupees [Proviso to section 17–A].

5.3.13 Provisions Relating to Jurisdiction [Section 17–B]

(1) No Court inferior to that of a [Metropolitan Magistrate of Judicial Magistrate of the first class] shall try any offence punishable under Section 17A [Section 17 B (1)].

(2) No prosecution for such offence shall be instituted, except by an Inspector with the previous sanction of the Welfare Commissioner [Section 17- B (2)].

(3) No Court shall take cognizance of such offence, unless complaint thereof is made within six months of the date on which the offence is alleged to have been committed [Section 17 B (3)].

5.3.14 Supersession of Board [Section 18]

(1) If the State Government is satisfied that the Board has made default in performing any duties imposed on it by or under this Act or has abused its, power, the State Government may by notification in the Official Gazette supersede and reconstitute the Board in the manner prescribed for constitution of the Board [Section 18 (1)].

It is provided that before issuing the notification under this sub-section, the State Government will give a reasonable opportunity to the Board to show cause why it should not be superseded and shall consider the explanations and objections, if any, of the Board [Proviso to Section 18 (2)].

(2) After the supersession of the Board and until it is reconstituted the powers, duties and functions of the Board under this Act shall be exercised or performed by the Board or by such officer or officers as the State Government may appoint for this purposes [Section 18 (2)].

5.3.15 Members of Board, Welfare Commissioner, Inspectors and all Officers and Servants of Board to be Public Servants under Section 20

"The members of the Board, the Welfare Commissioner, inspectors and all officers and servants of the Board, shall be deemed to be public servants within the meaning of Section 21 of the Indian Penal Code."

5.3.16 Protection to Persons Acting in Good Faith

No suit, prosecution or other legal proceedings shall lie against any, person for anything which is in good faith done or intended to be done under this Act [Section 21].

5.3.17 Exemption

The State Government may, after consulting the Board by notification in the Official Gazette exempt any class of establishment from all or any of the provisions of this Act subject to such conditions as may be specified in the notification [Section 22].

5.4 RULES MADE UNDER SECTION 19 OF THE M.L.W. FUND ACT OF 1953

Important Rules have been included in Section 19 of this Act for the purpose of carrying out the objective of the Act. These rules are as under.

(1) The State Government may, by notification in the Official Gazette and subject to the condition of previous publication, make rules to carry out the purposes of this Act [Section 19 (1)].

(2) In particular and without prejudice to the generality of the foregoing power, such rules may be made for all or any of the following matters namely,

(a) The intervals at which or the period within which any of the sums referred to in Section 3 shall be paid to the Board or into the Fund, the manner of making such payment and the agency for, and manner of, collection of any such sum.

(b) The manner in which the accounts of the Fund shall be maintained and audited under sub-section (3) of Section 3;

(c) The procedure for, making grants from the Fund under Section 7;

(d) The procedure for defraying the expenditure incurred in administering the Fund;

(e) The number of representatives of employer and employees, independent members and representatives of women on, the Board, and the allowances, if any, payable to them, under Section 4;

(f) The manner in which the Board shall conduct their business;

(g) The duties and powers of the Inspectors and the conditions of service of the Welfare Commissioner and inspectors appointed under this Act;

(h) The delegation of the powers and functions of the Board to the Welfare Commissioner and the conditions and limitations subject to which the powers may be exercised or functions discharged;

(i) The percentage of the annual income of the Fund beyond which the Board may not spend or, the staff and on other administrative members',

(j) The registers and records to be maintained and returns 'to be sent to the Board under this Act;

(k) The publication of the report of the activities financed from the Fund together with a statement of receipts and expenditures of the Fund and statement of accounts;

(l) Any other matter which under this Act is or may be prescribed [Section 19 (2)].

(3) Every rule made under this Act shall be laid, as soon as or may be after it, is made, before each house of the State Legislature while it is in session for a total period of thirty days which may be comprised in one session or in two successive sessions and if, before the expiry of the session in which it is so laid or the session immediately following, both Houses agree in making any modification in the rule or both Houses agree that the rule should not be made, the rule shall; from the date of publication of a notification in the Official Gazette of such decision, have effect only in such modified form, or be of no effect, as the case may be; so however that any such modification or annulment shall be without prejudice to the validity of, anything previously done or omitted to, be done under that rule [Section 19 (3)].

5.5 MEANING AND DEFINITIONS OF 'SOCIAL SECURITY'

The idea of social security originated in the realisation by the State of its responsibility to provide its citizens adequately against certain contingencies. In the past, the State contented itself by protecting its poor citizens against want and poverty. Sir William Beveridge rightly pointed out that "Want is only one of the five giants on the road of reconstruction, and in some ways, the easiest to attack, the others are Disease, Ignorance, Squalor and Idleness". The word 'Squalor' implies 'dirty and unpleasant'. Social security aims at providing protection against these big and dangerous giants.

The International Labour Organisation is basically responsible for the keen interest taken in and in the progress of social security in different states. The issue of social security has been on top of the agenda of the International Labour Organisation.

In simple words, *social security is the security that a society provides against certain risks to which its members are exposed.* Such security is usually provided through appropriate agencies or organisations. These risks are in fact essentially contingencies against which an individual cannot protect himself because of his small means. These contingencies include employment, injuries, sickness, disablement, industrial diseases, maternity, old age, widowhood, unemployment and so on.

The purpose of social security is to provide for such contingencies. The government usually takes steps to protect its citizens against these risks or contingencies. Social security really forms an important part of labour welfare providing security which is of great importance to the worker's and his family's well-being.

Many expert organisations in the field of labour welfare and social security, have defined the concept of social security. Let us consider a few definitions of 'social security' in order to understand the concept of social security.

(a) According to **Friedlander** "*Social security is a programmer of protection provided by society against the contingencies of modern life i.e. sickness, unemployment, old age, dependency, industrial accidents and invalidism against which the individual cannot be expected to protect himself and his family by his own ability or foresight*". The word invalidism used in this definition implies removal of a person from active service because of his ill health or injury caused to him.

(b) In **Encyclopaedia of Social Work** (Vol. I, page 280), it is mentioned that social security *is the endeavour of the community as a whole to render help to the utmost extent possible to any individual during periods of physical distress consequent on reduction or loss of earnings due to illness, disablement, maternity, unemployment, old age or death of working member.*

(c) According to **Weber** and **Cohen** social security is *a controversial and dynamic subject with various facets-philosophical, theoretical, humanitarian, financial, administrative, social, economic, political, actuarial, medical and legal.*

(d) An ILO seminar was held in New Delhi in September 1977 in which a more comprehensive definition of social security was stated which is given below.

"*Social security is the protection furnished by the society to its members through a series of public measures against economic and social distress that are caused due to absence of earnings or substantial reduction or stoppage of earnings resulting from sickness, maternity and employment injury (including occupational diseases), unemployment (including absence of employment) and underemployment, invalidity, destitution (means complete poverty), social disability and backwardness, old age and death, and further to provide health care, including preventive measures*".

(e) According to **Sir William Beveridge**, the term social security is used to denote *the security of income to take the place of earnings when they are interrupted by unemployment, sickness or accident, to provide for retirement through age, to provide for loss of support by the death of another person and to meet an exceptional expenditure such as those connected with birth, death and marriage.*

From the above mentioned definitions of social security, we have learnt certain aspects relating to social security which are as follows.

(1) There are certain contingent risks against which an individual, who has small means, cannot protect himself. Such contingent risks include employment, injury, sickness, industrial disease, disablement, widowhood, unemployment, accident etc. Therefore, social security measures are introduced to protect the individuals. The main purpose of social security is to provide an income up to a minimum and also medical treatment facilities to bring the interruption of earnings to an end as far as possible.

(2) Social security forms an important part of labour welfare providing the security which is of great importance from the point of view of well being of workers and their family.

(3) Social security can be provided either by way of insurance or assistance from the state.

(4) The coverage of social security is dynamic. In some countries, the term social security is applied to all governmental programmers planned to maintain incomes of certain groups of people. In other countries, it applies mainly to social insurance programmers. In certain countries, it covers a variety of health and welfare services.

(5) Though social security programmes vary from country to country, following are the three important characteristics of those programmes.

(a) The social security programmes are introduced by law,

(b) They provide some form of cash payment to individuals to replace at least a part of the lost income that occurs due to such contingencies as work injury, sickness, old age and death, unemployment etc.

(c) Social insurance, social assistance or public services are three important ways to provide benefits or services under social security measures.

(6) Generally, the government takes steps to protect the citizens against various risks, and contingencies. Employers, trade unions also can help in this respect to ease the financial and administrative burden.

(7) The concept of social security is based on ideals of human dignity and social justice. It is one of the measures to achieve the general objective of social welfare. The underlying idea behind social security measures is that a citizen who has contributed or is likely to contribute to his country's welfare should be given protection against certain hazards.

5.6 THE OBJECTIVES AND IMPORTANCE OF SOCIAL SECURITY AND SOCIAL SECURITY MEASURES

The basic objective of social security is to protect those people who are poor who cannot provide for various risks and contingencies. For this purpose, various social security measures are introduced.

These measures are essential because an individual cannot protect himself and his family against various risks such as accidents, occupational diseases, unemployment etc. by his own ability, foresight, hard work and so on. If nothing is done, these risks or contingencies imperil a working man's ability to support himself and his dependents decently and in a healthy manner. Hence, supplementary comprehensive measures are necessary. Such measures are introduced by the state or society.

The objective of the social security measures is three-fold i.e. compensation, restoration and prevention. Compensation is related to income security. It is based upon the idea that during spells of risks, the individuals and their families should not be subject to a double calamity involving destitution and loss of health, limbs, work, life etc. Restoration means cure of risks of sickness re-employment and rehabilitation. Preventive measures of social security help to increase the material intellectual and moral well-being of the people at work.

Social insurance, social assistance and public services are three important ways through which social security can be provided.

Medical care sickness benefits, maternity benefits, accidents benefits, unemployment benefit, old age and invalidity benefits etc. are the benefits which are normally provided under the social security schemes. From the view point of labour welfare, these benefits are very important which help to maintain and increase labour productivity.

Social security measures are very important as they improve morale of working class of the people by providing sense of security amongst them against various industrial hazards including unjustified dismissals. They introduce an element of stability and protection.

Social security does not protect merely the subscriber but it also protects his or her entire family by providing benefit packages in financial security and health care. Social security schemes are designed to guarantee long-term subsistence to the families when the earning members retire, die, or suffer disabilities.

It implies that the main strength of the social security system as a whole is that it acts as a facilitator. It helps the people to plan their future through social insurance and social assistance. For the success of social security measures, active support and involvement of employees and employers is essential.

On the whole, social security measures are significant from two view points. First, they constitute an important step toward the goal of welfare state. Secondly, these measures enable workers to become more efficient and thus reduce wastages. Lack of social security impedes production and prevents formation of a stable and efficient labour force. Hence, social security measures are not considered as a burden, but they are considered as a wise investment which yields good dividends.

In the report of the National Commission on Labour the importance of social security, it is stated in the report that, "Social security has become a fact of life and these measures have introduced an element of stability and protection in the midst of stresses and strains of modern life. It is a major aspect of public policy today and the extent of its prevalence is a measure of the progress made by a country towards the idea of a welfare state. It is an incentive for development, substituting as it does hope for fear in the process improving the efficiency of the working force".

5.7 SOCIAL SECURITY PROVISIONS IN INDIA

The Directive Principles of state policy as embodied in the constitution of India lay special stress on the goal of 'Welfare State' by directing the state to follow certain principles which are very essential to secure a social order for the promotion of welfare of the people. From this point of view, a number of social security legislations have been enacted from time to time.

In India, various factors contributed to the evolution of social security legislation. The growth of industrialisation exodus to the cities, disintegration of the joint family system increasing unemployment, poverty among the masses etc. are some such factors. Because of these factors, the individuals could not have access to the kind of resources needed to cope with unexpected risks. The change in the political, social atmosphere has also made a considerable impact. Therefore, many Acts have been passed in India for the provision of social security. These Acts can be broadly classified into the following two categories.

(I)   Acts that provide security in case of employment injury, maternity and sickness; and

(II) Acts that cover old age and unemployment. The following three important Acts come under the first category:

   (a) The Workmen's Compensation Act of 1923.

   (b) The Employee's State Insurance Act of 1948.

   (c) The Maternity Benefit Act of 1961.

   (d) The Plantations Labour Act of 1951.

The important which come under the second category are as follows :

   (i)   The Industrial Disputes Act of 1947.

   (ii) The Employee's Provident Funds and Miscellaneous Previsions Act of 1952.

   (iii) The Payment of Gratuity Act of 1972.

   (iv) The Seamen's Provident Fund Act of 1966,

   (v)   The Coal Mines Provident Fund and Bonus Schemes Act of 1948.

POINTS TO REMEMBER

- Labour welfare is one of the major aspects of national programmes towards bettering the working class and creating a comfortable work environment for them.

- Various welfare measures and activities are undertaken by the state government and association of workers increasing the standard of living and for the improvement of their economic and social well-being.

- Various labour welfare measures are introduced. Such measures can be classified into following two categories :

  (a) Voluntary or non-statutory labour welfare measures.

  (b) Statutory labour welfare measures.

- In Maharashtra, the Bombay Labour Welfare Fund Act was passed in 1953 in order to provide for the constitution of a labour welfare fund for the financing of activities to promote welfare of labour This Act is called as the Maharashtra Labour Welfare Fund Act, 1953.

- "An Act to provide for the constitution of a fund for the financing of activities to promote welfare of labour in the State of Maharashtra for conducting such activities and for certain other purposes."

- This Act has been passed to provide for the constitution of a fund for financing the activities to promote welfare of the labour/ workers in the State of Maharashtra.

- The Maharashtra Labour Welfare Board (M.L.W. Board) is the corporate body constituted under this Act. This Board is responsible for conducting various welfare activities according to the provisions of this Act.

- The idea of social security originated in the realisation by the State of its responsibility to provide its citizens adequately against certain contingencies.

- The International Labour Organisation is basically responsible for the keen interest taken and in the progress of social security in different states. The issue of social security has been on top of the priority agenda of the International Labour Organisation.

- Social security really forms an important part of labour welfare providing the security which is of great importance to the worker's and his family, is well-being.

- The basic objective of social security is to protect those people who are poor who cannot provide for various risks and contingencies.

- The objective of the social security measures is three-fold. i.e. compensation, restoration and prevention.
- Social insurance, social assistance and public services are three important ways through which social security can be provided.

QUESTIONS FOR DISCUSSION

Q.1   Explain important provisions of the M.L.W. Fund Act of 1953 relating to 'Labour Welfare Fund.

Q.2   Explain the object, application and scope of the M.L.W. Fund Act of 1953.

Q.3   Explain the constitution of Welfare Fund.

Q.4   What are the provisions of the Act relating to unpaid accumulations and claims there to?

Q.5   Explain the provision of the Act relating to contribution by an employer and an employee.

Q.6   How is the Welfare Fund vested and utilised?

Q.7   What are the provisions of the Act relating to the constitution of the M.L.W. Board under the Act?

Q.8   What are the provisions of the Act relating to appointment and powers of Welfare Commissioner?

Q.9   State and explain the dentition of social security.

Q.10   Explain the objectives and importance of social security.

Q.11   Write short notes on the following:

   (a)   The Labour Welfare Fund.

   (b)   The Maharashtra Labour Welfare Board.

   (c)   Powers of Welfare commissioner.

   (d)   Meaning of social security.

   (e)   Objective and importance of social security.

QUESTIONS FROM PREVIOUS EXAMINATIONS

Q.1   Discuss the merits and demerits of rising urbanisation in developing countries due to rapid industrialisation and its impact on social health.   **[Dec-2012]**

Q.2   State and Explain the relation between Mental, Physical, Social and Industrial Health from Labour Welfare point of view.   **[April-2010]**

Q.3   Write Short Notes on:

(a)   The Relationship of Welfare to Productivity.   **[Dec-2010]**

(b)   Social Security.   **[April-2011]**

UNIVERSITY QUESTION PAPER
April 2015

Time : 2 ¹/₂ Hours   **Maximum Marks : 50**

Instructions ...

(i)   *All questions are compulsory.*

(ii)   *Each question has an internal option.*

(iii) *Each question carries 10 marks.*

(iv)   *Figures to the right indicate full marks for that question/sub-question.*

(v)   *Your answers should be specific and to the point.*

---

1. (a) Define Labour Welfare. Give the objectives and principles of the existence of labour welfare   **(10)**

OR

   (b) Introduce ILO and ILC with its objectives and structure.   **(10)**

2. (a) What are the various roles and duties performed by a Labour Welfare Officer. **(10)**

OR

   (b) Are the roles and duties of a Personnel Manager same as to the Labour Welfare Officer.   **(10)**

3. (a) Describe the role of Government in Labour Welfare Activities.   **(10)**

OR

   (b) Does the trade unions and NGOs extend a helping hand towards the labour welfare activities in various sectors of industry ?   **(10)**

4. (a) Write a note on Workers Education Scheme.   **(10)**

OR

   (b) Productivity and integration are linked with workers participation in management. Comment.   **(10)**

5. (a) Labour welfare is related to the mental, social and physical health of an employee. Comment.   **(10)**

OR

   (b) Write a note on theories of labour welfare.   **(10)**

✍ ✍ ✍
